The Secret
at Seven Rocks

As Nancy inched her way carefully over the slippery rocks and mud of the mountainside, she wondered who had abducted her and why. There was a sudden snap as the heel of one of her shoes broke. Then her foot slid out from under her, and she was tumbling head over heels down the mountain.

Nancy came to a thumping stop, lying facedown on the wet earth. She rolled over onto her side and winced at the pain in her knee, where she had hit it on a sharp rock. "Things can't get much worse than this," Nancy said to herself.

A low growl told her she had spoken too soon.

Slowly, Nancy lifted her head to stare into the eyes of a very large cinnamon-colored bear.

Nancy Drew
Mystery Stories

Available from MINSTREL Books

THE SECRET AT SEVEN ROCKS

CAROLYN KEENE

PUBLISHED BY POCKET BOOKS

New York   London   Toronto   Sydney   Tokyo   Singapore

A MINSTREL PAPERBACK *ORIGINAL*

 A Minstrel Book, published by
POCKET BOOKS, a division of Simon & Schuster
1230 Avenue of the Americas, New York, NY 10020

ISBN: 0-671-69285-2

First Minstrel Books printing February 1991

10   9   8   7   6   5   4   3

NANCY DREW, NANCY DREW MYSTERY STORIES,
A MINSTREL BOOK and colophon are registered trademarks
of Simon & Schuster.

Cover art by Aleta Jenks

Printed in the U.S.A.

Contents

THE SECRET AT
SEVEN ROCKS

1

A Perfect Day for Hiking

Nancy Drew raised the window, opened the white wooden shutters, and took a deep breath of pine-scented air. "This is heaven!" she said, her blue eyes gazing out at the majestic Rocky Mountains, rising behind the village of Seven Rocks. A soft breeze blew back her reddish blond shoulder-length hair.

"That may be heaven," agreed her friend George Fayne, nodding toward the window. "But this," she said, pointing to the bed where her cousin Bess was sorting camping gear, "is a mess."

Bess Marvin glanced at the small red day pack on the bed in front of her, then at the mound of supplies spread out next to it. "How will I fit everything into this little pack?" she asked.

"Bess," said George, neatly zipping her own pack closed, "we're only going on a short hike. All you need is a bottle of fresh drinking water and the sandwiches we made this morning. What is all that stuff, anyway?"

Bess frowned as she ran a hand through her straw blond hair. "Well, there's my compass, water bottle, snakebite kit, bug repellent, sun block, beach towel, first-aid kit, Swiss Army knife, hairbrush, emergency thermal blanket—"

"Nancy, help," moaned George.

Across the room, Nancy was still gazing at the mountains. Caught up in the view, she'd only been half-listening to her two closest friends. "What's the matter?" she asked.

George pointed to Bess's gear.

"I was only in the Girl Scouts for two weeks," Bess said, "but I remember they always said to be prepared."

"That's the Boy Scouts," George told her.

"It doesn't matter," Bess insisted. "You never know what will happen—especially when you're with Nancy Drew."

Nancy laughed. "Am I that awful to travel with?"

"Not awful," said George, smiling. "Just . . . exciting."

Although she was only eighteen, Nancy Drew had been solving mysteries for as long as Bess and

George could remember. In their hometown of River Heights, the police knew the young detective so well that they often called on her for help. Bess and George had learned that even when they were away from home, mysteries had a way of finding Nancy.

"This time," Nancy said, "all I want is a nice, boring vacation. Hiking in the mountains, maybe watching a sunrise . . ."

George and Bess gave each other alarmed looks. They weren't crazy about getting up that early.

"All right. You can skip the sunrise," Nancy said with a laugh. "But let's get on with the hiking." She walked over to the bed and peered into Bess's overflowing pack. "Well, you'll have more room in here if you get rid of Munro," she said. She reached in and lifted a large, sleepy, orange-striped cat from the bottom of the pack. "I think we can probably do without the beach towel, too," Nancy suggested.

"And the emergency blanket," George added.

Bess sat down on the bed with a sigh. "Why did I ever agree to this?" she wondered aloud. "I don't even like hiking."

Blue-eyed Bess and her cousin George, who had dark eyes and hair, couldn't have been more different. George, a natural athlete, was tall and slim and never seemed to gain an ounce. Bess, who loved food and hated exercise, was always slightly overweight. Nancy and George practically had to beg her to join them on their hike in the Rockies. Now Nancy wanted to be sure her friend had a good time.

"Think of this vacation as two weeks at a free spa," Nancy said. "After all, you keep saying you want to lose five pounds. And here we are, staying in a beautiful old Victorian house in the historic town of Seven Rocks. We've got nothing to do except go hiking in the gorgeous Colorado Rockies."

"Aren't spas supposed to be relaxing?" Bess asked. "You know . . . hot tubs, saunas, mud baths?"

Nancy looked around at the gracious, airy bedroom that the three of them were sharing. The Larsen house had been built in the 1860s, and though it had running water and electricity, it was a long way from having a hot tub or a sauna. Nancy tried to think of something that would cheer up Bess. "I know," she said. "Maybe tomorrow we can check out some of those antique shops in town."

"Definitely," Bess said, sounding more enthusiastic. "I saw one that looks like it has some great vintage dresses. It'll be perfect for Gaslight Night. You know, that night when everyone in town gets decked out in Victorian clothing." Bess loved clothes almost as much as Nancy loved mysteries.

4

"So much for hiking and getting in shape," George teased.

"Come on," Nancy said, shouldering her own pack. "We're missing the nicest part of the day."

Bess hurriedly finished packing and followed Nancy and George down the long, curving staircase of the spacious home.

Nancy led the way to the small sunny room that Maggie Larsen had turned into an office. Maggie and her husband, Cal, were good friends of Nancy's father, Carson Drew. The three had all gone to college together. Although Nancy's father and the Larsens didn't see one another often, their friendship had remained strong. At the last minute, Carson Drew had been unable to make the trip to Colorado with Nancy. Bess and George had been only too happy to join Nancy for two weeks in the Rockies.

Maggie sat at her computer, her fingers flying over the keyboard. A friendly, energetic woman in her forties, Maggie worked at home, writing hiking and tourist guides for the area around Seven Rocks.

"Be with you in a minute," she said. "Just let me finish this paragraph."

Nancy couldn't help thinking that Maggie, who wore her long gray hair swept up into a twist, was the perfect person to live in a Victorian house. She always looked both elegant and casual, as if she'd be equally comfortable in faded jeans or a floor-length dress.

"Well," Maggie said, turning away from the computer, "it looks as if you three are ready for your first Rocky Mountain hike. Would you like a suggestion for a trail?"

"Please," said Nancy.

Munro, who had followed the girls down from the bedroom, jumped onto Maggie's lap and began meowing in earnest.

"I think he's complaining," Bess said. "He was sleeping in my pack, and we threw him out."

"He'll get over it," Maggie assured her, scratching the cat behind his ear. "Actually, I think he was saying that you're all flatlanders. You ought to give yourselves some time to adjust to the elevation before you take on anything too steep."

"Sounds good to me," Bess said quickly.

Maggie smiled. "The altitude really isn't that much of a problem. But we're about six thousand feet above sea level here. You may find yourselves running out of breath or getting thirsty quicker than usual. Just take it slow, and you'll be fine."

Maggie reached over to an oak bookcase and pulled out a map and one of the paperback guides she'd written. Unfolding the map on her desk, she pointed to the Cloud Lake trail. "This will give you a nice, gentle start. It's a well-marked trail that leads to Cloud Lake. You're so lucky to be here in the fall. The quaking aspens have just turned gold!"

"Even what we can see of the mountains from here is beautiful," Nancy agreed.

"You're in for a treat," Maggie promised. "Seven Rocks is a fine little town, but nothing beats actually being up in the mountains. Here, take the guide with you," she offered. "It will help if you want to identify trees or birds. And make sure you each have a jacket. Weather changes quickly in high elevations."

"Check," said George. "Thanks to Bess, we're carrying nearly everything we brought for the next two weeks."

Bess glared at her cousin, and Nancy broke in quickly before the argument could start up again. "Thanks, Maggie," she said. "We'll be back by evening."

Maggie winked at them. "Just watch out for wild animals."

"Exactly what kind of wild animals do you think Maggie was talking about?" Bess asked a little breathlessly as the three friends walked along the winding mountain trail.

"Lions and tigers and bears," George teased.

"Well, there *are* black bears in the Rockies,"

Nancy said, glancing at the guidebook she held. "And mountain lions. But according to Maggie's guide here, both lions and bears do their best to avoid people. And considering that we've already seen about ten other hikers on this trail, it's probably not a favorite with bears and mountain lions."

"Well, I know why people like it here so much," George said. "It's got to be one of the most gorgeous places on earth."

It was a perfectly clear day, and the mountains were as beautiful as Maggie had promised. Blue spruce, ponderosa and piñon pine edged the trail. Birds were calling to one another as if it were the first day of spring.

All three girls were feeling a little winded, but no one wanted to stop. At every bend in the winding trail, the Rockies seemed to open up some new secret to them: a waterfall racing over craggy cliffs, a meadow filled with wildflowers, or just a break in the trees where the vast blue western sky made even the Rockies look small.

Suddenly, the trail opened onto a stand of quaking aspen. The tall, golden trees looked as if they were ablaze with sunlight. And just beyond the trees stood a small herd of mule deer. The deer gazed at the three girls calmly, flicking their large, rounded ears.

"I guess we've seen our wild animals," George said softly. "Look how big their eyes are."

"They're lovely," Bess said, moving quietly to the edge of the trail. "I'll bet the little ones were born this spring."

One of the youngest deer looked at the girls curiously and then cautiously started toward them. All three girls stood as still as they could, not wanting to startle it.

"How close do you think it will come?" Bess breathed.

Nancy never got a chance to answer. Instead, the deafening crack of a gunshot ripped through the woods. The deer scattered at once.

Then Nancy heard George scream, "Bess! Are you okay?"

2

A Missing Bear

Nancy rushed to Bess's side. "Bess!" she cried. "Are you hurt?"

"Relax," Bess said, grinning up at Nancy and George. "I just got startled by the gunshot and lost my balance. I wasn't hit or anything."

"Are you sure?" George asked.

"Positive." Bess sat up and brushed herself off. "Are the deer okay?"

Nancy stood up and looked into the aspens. "I think so. They've all scattered. Still, that shot came awfully close to us." She turned and scanned the trees behind them. There was no sign of anyone. On instinct, she headed toward the darkest part of the woods.

"Where are you going?" George asked, setting off after her. Bess was close behind.

"To find out who fired that gun," Nancy replied. She stopped and waited for her friends. "Whoever it is could have hit one of us. He ought to be told he's firing into a hiking trail before he takes a second shot."

"Nancy," Bess said nervously, "we really shouldn't go off the trail. I mean—"

"We'll go with you," George interrupted.

Moving carefully, Nancy made her way deeper into the woods. She was glad that George and Bess had chosen to come with her.

Suddenly, they heard a high-pitched yowl. It wasn't very loud, and it was coming from somewhere on the ground. Nancy's eyes searched the dense tangle of plants and roots. Then a movement on the forest floor caught her attention.

A small spotted cat with big rounded ears gazed up at her. It opened its mouth and hissed.

Nancy stepped back, startled. The cat also tried to back up, but there was something wrong with its right rear leg. It limped and cried out in pain.

"You're hurt," Nancy said, kneeling a short distance away from the cat. The little animal hissed again, warning her not to come any closer.

"A kitten!" Bess cried, coming up behind Nancy. "It's so cute."

11

"That's no kitten," George said, sounding slightly alarmed. "That's a baby mountain lion!"

"Are you sure?" Nancy asked. "I didn't think mountain lions had spots."

"Adults don't," George said, consulting Maggie's book. "'Mountain lions,'" she read, "'are also known as cougars, pumas, and catamounts. The cubs keep their spots for about six months. They are easy to recognize by the dark, almost triangular marks along the sides of the muzzle.'" She looked up from the book and frowned at the cub. "That's definitely a baby mountain lion."

"Was it shot?" Bess asked.

"Let me look," Nancy answered. "I see blood on its leg. It looks like a fresh wound. That reckless hunter must have shot it and left it here, helpless. It can't even get away from us."

Bess dropped down beside the cub for a closer look. Immediately, she jumped back as the cat tried to rake her with its claws. "I don't think it wants to be touched," she said in a shaky voice.

"It's terrified," George said, stooping over the cat. "It looks like the leg bone has been nicked slightly. I don't think the bullet went in very deep. But still, the little guy has lost some blood."

Nancy rocked back on her heels. "It won't be easy, but we've got to get it to a veterinarian.

Otherwise, it will starve or be eaten itself. Besides, it's probably in a great amount of pain."

George shook her head doubtfully. "I tried to pick up an alley cat once. It nearly clawed me to death. Picking up a wounded mountain lion—even a baby—is not a good idea."

"Well, we can't leave it here," Nancy said. She took off her jacket. Carefully, she wrapped the jacket around the cub, making sure to stay clear of its teeth and claws.

The little mountain lion hissed and tried to snap at her. "Don't be frightened," Nancy said in a soothing voice. "I'm not going to hurt you." She stood up and turned to her friends. "Let's get back to town as quickly as we can."

"What about the gunshot?" George asked.

In the excitement of finding the cub, Nancy had completely forgotten about searching for whoever had fired the gun. Some detective I am, she thought ruefully. Then she looked at the squirming bundle in her arms and knew what her decision had to be. "I guess that question will have to wait," she said.

Although George drove as fast as she could within the speed limit, the drive back to Seven Rocks seemed to take forever. Nancy sat beside George, holding the cub and murmuring to it in a

13

soothing tone. The cub stared at her with huge dark eyes, its small body trembling. "Just a little while longer," she told it.

Finally, George turned onto the curving, tree-lined street where the Larsens lived.

Minutes later, the girls found Maggie in the kitchen preparing a salad. "I didn't expect you back so early," she said with surprise. "Cal is due home for a late lunch soon. Why don't you join us? We can—" She broke off as she saw what Nancy was carrying. "My, my," she said softly. "Where did you find this one?"

Nancy gently set the cub on the table and explained what had happened.

"You can bet that shot came from a hunter who was after those deer," Maggie said angrily. "The fall hunting season just started. Every fool with a shotgun is out there, tearing up the woods. Usually, though, they have sense enough to stay clear of the hiking trails." She stopped as the cub gave a soft cry. "I'd better call Dr. Hutchins, the vet," she said briskly.

Nancy stayed with the cub until Maggie returned a few minutes later, a worried expression on her face. "Dr. Hutchins is on vacation for the next two weeks," she said.

"Is there another veterinarian in town?" Nancy asked.

14

"Not in Seven Rocks," Maggie answered. "You'd have to drive a good seventy-five miles to the next town for another one. But there is Paws."

"Paws?" Nancy echoed.

"It's a wildlife rehabilitation center about twenty miles up the mountain," Maggie explained. "Dana Walsh runs it. What they do there is take in injured animals, nurse them back to health, and then release them back into the wild. Dana's not a full-fledged vet, of course, but she and the people who work with her have had special training and lots of experience. I'm sure they can deal with this."

Nancy looked at the little mountain lion again. It had grown much quieter since she'd brought it into the house. Was it calmer or just weaker? she wondered. "We'll try Paws," she told Maggie.

Once again, Maggie took out a map and gave the girls directions. She was just finishing when the kitchen door opened and Cal Larsen came in, looking unusually worried. A warm, easygoing man with a round face and a gray mustache, Cal was chief of the news desk for Seven Rocks' daily paper, the *Sentinel*.

"Sorry I'm late, Maggie," he said, kissing his wife on the cheek. "A hot story just came in over the wire. We had to rearrange the entire front page."

"What is it this time?" Maggie asked.

15

"A prison break late last night," Cal said grimly. "From the federal penitentiary in Griffin."

"But that's over two hundred miles away," Maggie said.

"Yes, but five prisoners escaped," her husband said. "None have been found yet, as far as we know. The five men could be headed in different directions. This story is going to be front-page news all over the country." Suddenly, Cal noticed the three girls gathered around the map. "Aren't you all supposed to be hiking?" he asked in a joking tone. "And why is there a mountain lion on my kitchen table?"

Maggie quickly explained what had happened. Cal muttered something angrily about careless hunters and then offered to drive the girls up to Paws.

"Thanks," Nancy said, "but Maggie just gave us great directions. I'm sure we'll find it. I think we ought to leave right now, though. This little fellow has to be fixed up."

Bess navigated as George drove the yellow rental car up the mountain. Paws wasn't that far from town, but most of the route consisted of narrow, winding mountain roads. Nancy sat with the lion cub on her lap, feeling its heart racing furiously beneath her hand. "I can't fix your leg," she told it,

"but I wish I could get you to stop being so afraid."
The trembling cat gave a high-pitched cry.

"There!" Bess said, pointing to a wooden sign that read Paws.

George slowed the car and turned onto a tree-lined gravel road. After about two miles, they passed two tall pillars on either side of the road. Another mile beyond that, they passed a deserted stone gate house. In the distance, the girls could see a huge three-story house made of the same gray fieldstone.

"Maggie didn't say this was an old estate," Bess said, sounding slightly awed.

"Someone must have had a lot of money and a craving for privacy," Nancy observed.

George pulled to a stop in front of the main house. Immediately, the front door opened, and a boy wearing a blue T-shirt and jeans came down the steps. He must have been about nineteen, Nancy guessed. He was slim and wiry and very tanned, with short dark hair. He had an intense expression on his face as he approached the car.

"What are you doing here?" he demanded. "This is private property."

"We're looking for Dana Walsh," Nancy said.

"She isn't here," he said flatly. "You'd better leave."

Nancy bit back an angry retort and instead held up the cub, who gave a low cry. "We found it on a trail," she said. "It's been shot in the leg."

The boy's attitude changed at once. "Let me see it," he said gently, his gray eyes concerned.

Somewhat reluctantly, Nancy got out of the car and handed him the cub. He laid it on the ground and examined it with deft, sure fingers. Nancy couldn't help being impressed. The cat stopped trembling almost as soon as the boy touched it.

"The bone has been grazed by a bullet," he said, looking up at Nancy. "I can wrap it and splint it, but the cub should stay here for a few weeks until the wound mends. Unless you have a pen for it, that is."

"No, we don't," Nancy said, glancing at Bess and George, who had gotten out of the car. "It'd be great if you could keep the cub here. By the way, what is your charge?"

The boy stood up, gently cradling the cub. "None. Dana runs this place as a charity." Then he turned and headed back toward the house.

"Wait!" Nancy said, not ready to completely give up the young cub. "Can I come see it again?"

The boy frowned. "That's not a good idea," he said.

"Jesse!" a female voice said sharply. "You don't have to be so rude." Jesse continued walking, his full attention now on the cub.

Nancy turned in surprise to see a young woman of about twenty-five stepping out from the woods that bordered the estate. She was wearing jeans, hiking boots, and a plaid flannel shirt. Her long brown hair fell to her waist in a single, thick braid.

"Dana Walsh," said the woman, holding out her hand. Nancy liked her at once. "I apologize for Jesse," Dana went on. "I'm afraid he's not very friendly."

"You can say that again," George muttered.

Nancy looked back toward Jesse, but the boy was gone. "I'm Nancy Drew," she said quickly. "And these are my friends, George Fayne and Bess Marvin."

"What was wrong with the cub?" Dana asked.

Nancy explained about the cub's leg and the gunshot she and the girls had heard.

Dana's face turned red in anger when she heard about the hunters. "The situation has got to end," she said. "The woods are becoming a combat zone." She sighed and looked at Nancy. "I'm glad you all weren't hurt. And despite the bad impression he made, Jesse is very good with animals," Dana assured them. "I promise you the cub will get the best of care."

Nancy nodded. "It did seem to calm down the minute he touched it."

"That's Jesse's gift," Dana said. "Why don't you

let me make up for his bad manners and give you a tour of the grounds?''

"That would be terrific,'' Bess said eagerly. "This place is really something.''

Dana led the girls around the side of the main house. "I grew up down in Seven Rocks. I've only lived here the last three years.''

George gave a low whistle of admiration. "You bought this property for the refuge?''

Dana shook her head, smiling. "The estate belonged to my grandmother, who was a very eccentric lady. She cared more for animals than people, I think. When she died, she left this place to me and my brother. There was a strict provision that it be set up as a wildlife rehabilitation center. Her money is being used to care for animals and fight for their rights.''

"Wow,'' Bess said, "you and Jesse don't look anything alike.''

Dana laughed. "He's not my brother. Jesse just works here. He stays in the guest cottage over there.'' She pointed to a small stone cottage off to the side of the main house. "My brother, Steve, is older than I am. He's in California now, doing marine research. Grandmother never believed that Steve would leave the Rockies for the ocean— though he tried to tell her.''

"So you run this place by yourself?" Nancy asked.

"Luckily, I'm as crazy about animals as my grandmother was. I've always wanted to do this kind of work. And I love it here."

Dana led the girls into an open area where a feed shed and a number of wire-enclosed pens had been set up. A few of the pens were empty, but most held animals. Nancy smiled as she saw a young mule deer, a pygmy owl, a badger, and a coyote who was curled up, asleep. A small path led through the woods to another clearing, which contained much larger cages.

"In there is Jesse's pride and joy," Dana said. She pointed straight back to a roomy caged area that enclosed several large boulders.

Nancy caught her breath. She was looking at a great tawny mountain lion. The big cat paced its compound restlessly, a bandage wrapped around its middle. As the girls approached, it let out a furious growl.

"Is that what our cute little cub is going to grow into?" Bess asked in alarm.

"Don't take it personally," Dana told them. "Jesse's the only one she tolerates."

Nancy headed toward a large pen on the other end of the clearing. It contained a dish of water and an empty feeding bowl. The door to the pen was open, and the pen was empty.

"Dana," Nancy called. "What kind of animal is staying in here?"

"That's our—" Dana's face turned pale and her eyes opened wide. "Oh no!" she cried. "The black bear is loose!"

3

The Ghost of the Midnight Mine

"Why would anyone do this?" Dana asked in stunned disbelief. "That animal was injured."

"How do you know someone let it go?" Nancy asked. "Could the bear have gotten out on its own?"

"No," Dana said, looking distracted. "I fed the animal only a few hours ago. I fastened the latch myself and then stood there and watched the bear eat."

Nancy could feel her heart quicken. "Maybe we can help," she said.

Dana gave a short, humorless laugh. "I've got to call my volunteers and start searching the woods. That bear was a bad-tempered animal to begin with. We've got to find it before someone else does.

I don't even want to think about what it might do if it's still hurting." She looked at the three girls and shook her head. "I'd ask you to join the search, but you're not trained to—"

"Nancy's a detective," George put in. "She may be able to figure out what happened."

"I'm sure she can help you," Bess added.

"Well, that would be great," Dana agreed. "Look, I've got to call the others now. Will you be all right if I leave you here? I can send Jesse out to help you."

"That's all right," Nancy said quickly. "I'd rather look around on my own, if that's okay."

"Fine," Dana called. She was already heading back to the house. "Let me know what you find."

Nancy examined the pen closely. There were no obvious clues. She looked at the fastening device. It was simple to open—a matter of unfastening a latch and twisting a few wires. A bear couldn't spring the latch, but any person could have opened the pen easily.

George must have read her thoughts. "It's meant to keep an animal inside, not a human out."

"Exactly," Nancy said. Her gaze swept the huge compound. "Why don't we split up?" she suggested. "That way, we can check the entire compound and the area around the house for clues.

24

Then we'll meet back here." Bess and George readily agreed.

Twenty-five minutes later, Nancy was the first one back at the bear pen. She hadn't found a thing. Except for the bear cage, everything at Paws seemed orderly and undisturbed. She jumped a little as the mountain lion growled behind her. "You're no help," she told it. Frustrated, she stared at the bear pen once more. Then she noticed something she hadn't seen before—a folded slip of paper nearly buried by wood chips on the side of the pen.

She knelt and picked it up, then quickly put it in her pocket as she heard footsteps approaching.

"Why are you snooping around?" Jesse demanded.

Nancy stood up angrily. "Someone released a black bear from this pen," she told him. "I'm trying to find out who did it." She hesitated a moment. "Maybe you know something about it."

Jesse shot her an impatient look. "Listen," he said, "I nearly got my hand torn off trying to bandage that bear's wound. The last thing I'd do is mess with an animal like that when it's still hurt. If you knew what was good for you, you'd get out of here right now." He looked at her menacingly. Behind her, Nancy could hear the cat's low hiss.

Jesse stopped as Bess's cheerful voice floated into the clearing. "Find anything, Nancy?"

"Only our friend Jesse," Nancy called back just as cheerfully.

Jesse glared at her for a moment, then pushed past her. Nancy watched as he crouched in front of the mountain lion's cage, talking to it in a low, soothing voice. The big cat gave one last fierce growl. Then it sat on its haunches, its golden eyes fixed on the boy.

"George is waiting for us in the car," Bess reported. "We didn't find a thing."

"I'll meet you in the car in five minutes, Bess. I have to talk to Dana. Is she still in the house?" Nancy asked Jesse.

"No," Jesse replied without looking up at Nancy. "She's out looking for the bear."

Nancy circled the compound quickly but couldn't find Dana anywhere to show her the note. Not feeling welcome with only Jesse at the compound, Nancy decided she'd call Dana when she got back to the Larsens'.

As the girls drove back to Seven Rocks, Nancy carefully unfolded the slip of paper she'd found beside the cage. Centered on the page was a slightly smudged charcoal sketch of a cat. The cat was sitting tall, staring straight ahead. Nancy felt herself shiver. Although it was crudely drawn, there was something menacing about the cat. It looked as if it were waiting to attack. And beneath the cat were two short sentences:

I found you. Now I'm going to take you apart.

"Well, did you find Paws?" Maggie asked as the three girls entered the house. She was sitting at the dining room table, proofreading one of her manuscripts.

"That and more," Nancy answered, sinking into a comfortable wing chair.

At the tone in Nancy's voice, Maggie looked up from her work and frowned. "What's wrong?"

"We met Jesse, for starters," George told her.

"I see," Maggie said thoughtfully. "I suppose you discovered that Jesse McKay is not the world's friendliest person."

"But he is kind of cute," Bess admitted. "He's got those light gray eyes and—"

"Bess!" George scolded. "He practically threw us off the property."

Nancy framed her question carefully. "Maggie, can you think of anyone who'd have a reason to threaten Dana Walsh? Or Jesse McKay?"

Maggie took off her reading glasses and laughed. "I'm not sure who would want to threaten Jesse, but

27

probably half the population of Seven Rocks would like to threaten Dana. But that doesn't include Jesse. After all, Dana's the one who's given him a place to live and work he loves."

"Why would anyone want to hurt Dana?" Bess wondered. "She seems so nice."

"Dana's a lovely girl," Maggie said. "But at the moment she's got the entire town in an uproar. You see, Dana is very active in the animal rights movement. She's started a campaign in Seven Rocks to outlaw hunting. Cal and I are behind her one hundred percent, but there are a lot of people in this town who make their money during hunting season."

"Like the gun shops?" George asked.

"Well, there's only one gun shop in town," Maggie said. "But there's also a fairly large hunting outfit that takes out-of-towners into the mountains and guarantees them a kill. And anyone who benefits from tourists—the hotels and restaurants, even gas stations—welcomes hunting season."

Bess shivered. "It's an awful way to make money."

"As you and I see it," Maggie agreed. "But Seven Rocks is a small town without any real industry. Almost all of its business stems from the things that draw tourists: hiking, skiing, mountain climbing, the town's historic sights, and hunting. No one wants to stop money from coming in.

"And then there's the question of why people hunt," Maggie went on. "Some people hunt to feed their families. What they're doing isn't that different from buying a steak in the supermarket. But Dana's campaign is about outlawing hunting as a sport. In fact, she's holding a rally in the town park tomorrow at one o'clock. If you really want to know what it's all about, you should stop by."

"I think that's a good idea," Nancy said. Then she told Maggie what had happened at Paws.

That night, Nancy lay in bed, staring at the stars that shone through the window. Munro was snuggled up at the foot of the bed, purring loudly. Across the room, Bess and George were sound asleep. But Nancy couldn't keep her mind off several troubling questions: Who was the note written to? Dana? Who had written the note? And if so, why was this person threatening her?

The next morning Nancy came downstairs to find George, Bess, and the Larsens already eating breakfast on the veranda.

"Good morning, sleepyhead," said Cal. "And I thought you were an early riser."

"Not today," Nancy said, blushing a little. It had

taken her a long time to fall asleep the night before. The more she'd thought about what had happened at the refuge, the more convinced she was that Dana was in danger. She had tried to call Dana the night before, but the phone at Paws had been busy all evening. Earlier that morning, Nancy had tried again, but there was no answer.

"So," Maggie said, "what's on the agenda for today?"

"Actually, we thought we might go to the rally," Nancy said.

"That might be exciting," Cal said, standing up and squinting at the blue-gray sky. "But it's kind of overcast. The rally might get rained out." He winked at his wife. "Maybe the girls should visit old Phineas."

"Oh, Cal, go to work!" said Maggie, laughing.

"Who's Phineas?" George asked as Cal headed for his car.

"Phineas Josiah Armbruster opened the Midnight Silver Mine in 1885," Maggie explained. "He claimed that he dreamed the location of the silver one night exactly as the clock struck midnight. He picked a spot on the upper slope of the mountain that rises behind town. Anyway, the Midnight was Seven Rocks' only successful mine. It yielded silver for about two years. Then, in the winter of '87, a snowslide sealed the mine—with Phineas and three of his miners inside. They recovered the bodies that spring, but no one was ever able to get another ounce of silver out of that mine."

"And Cal wants us to go there?" Bess said, looking slightly anxious.

"He was only teasing," Maggie assured her. "At least once a year, someone sights Phineas's ghost at the mine. Always at midnight. Cal called the *Sentinel* this morning. Harry, a reporter, said there was another sighting last night." Maggie stood up and began to clear the dishes from the table. "Needless to say, Cal decided the ghost was *not* front-page news."

"I've always liked ghost stories," George said. "Let's go up to the mine and check it out."

Nancy looked at her friend and smiled. Ghosts didn't scare Nancy, either. She had investigated more than one haunted house, and she'd never found a real ghost. But often she'd found that when people reported ghosts, there really *was* something unusual going on. "I think that'd be a perfect thing to do before the rally," she said.

"Nancy!" Bess wailed.

"It's all right," Nancy said quickly. "If you don't want to come, you can hang out here and meet us at the rally."

"No," Bess said loyally. "I'm not abandoning you guys. Count me in."

"Well, here we are," Bess said nervously. The three girls were standing in front of the brass memorial to Phineas Josiah Armbruster. Behind them rose the seven huge granite cliffs that gave the town of Seven Rocks its name. Yesterday, Nancy had thought it one of the most spectacular settings she'd ever seen. But today, under gloomy skies, there was something forbidding about the cliffs, especially here on this deserted mountain slope. Nancy wasn't afraid of ghosts, but she, too, felt strangely uneasy, as if someone were watching her.

Directly in front of the girls was a low, boarded-up structure that had once led into the mine. The mine itself had been closed years ago. Now there was just a series of illustrated signs, telling the story of the Midnight Mine.

George read the signs quickly and frowned. "You mean we can't even go in?"

"That's fine with me," Bess said. "Don't you know these mine shafts were always caving in on people?"

A cool wind blew through the fir trees. "You've got a point," Nancy told Bess. Nancy walked around the area carefully, searching for any signs of the "ghost." The ground was littered with the usual

32

assortment of gum wrappers, cigarette butts, and bottle tops left by other tourists.

"I hate to say it," George said, "but I don't see anything unusual here."

"Neither do I," Nancy admitted. "I'm not even sure what it is I'm looking for. I can't help feeling there's something I'm overlooking, though."

"Shopping," Bess said firmly. "We've been in Seven Rocks for over twenty-four hours and we haven't been in one store! We haven't checked out that ice-cream parlor, either."

"All right," Nancy agreed, laughing. "We'll go back to town and go shopping until the rally starts."

The girls got back into the car with Nancy behind the wheel. She was pulling away from the mine when she suddenly slammed on the brakes.

"What is it?" George asked.

"I just looked in my rearview mirror," Nancy answered, "and I swear I saw a man wearing a long coat go into the mine!"

4

A Threat

Nancy put the car in reverse and drove straight back to the abandoned silver mine. Seconds later, she stopped the car and got out. She was determined to find whoever it was she'd seen entering the mine.

But there was no one. The boarded-up entrance was still covered with the same cobwebs the girls had seen earlier. Except for the sounds of Bess and George getting out of the car, the Midnight Mine was completely silent.

"I know I saw someone," Nancy said. "A man wearing a long coat and a hat. It looked like he walked straight into the mine."

"How?" George asked. "There's no way he could have gotten in without prying off these boards."

34

"Unless it was Phineas," Bess said in a small voice.

"Nope. He only comes out at midnight," George joked.

Nancy shook her head. "This guy was real, I'm sure of it. There has to be a good explanation for how he vanished." She searched the area one last time and then gave up. "All right, Bess," she said. "I think I'm ready for someplace tame. How about that ice-cream parlor?"

Nancy scooped the last bit of her mocha ice-cream soda from the tall frosted glass. "That's exactly what I needed," she said with satisfaction.

"Me, too," Bess agreed. "This is much better than that creepy old mine."

George glanced at her watch. "The rally's about to start," she said.

The three girls paid for their ice cream and headed for the town park. It was easy to find the rally. They followed the crowds heading toward the bandstand in the center of the park. Posters had been put up on most of the trees. One of them showed two tiny spotted mountain lion cubs. Beneath their picture were the words, "Yesterday their mother was shot." Nancy winced, thinking of the cub they'd found.

"Look at all these people!" George said in amazement. "You'd think it was a rock concert."

Just then a bearded man handed Nancy a flier about stopping hunting in Seven Rocks. Moments later, an elegantly dressed woman handed her another flier. It said that hunting was a legal activity that helped control wildlife populations.

Before Nancy could read much of either one, Dana Walsh took the stage. "Anyone who has ever had a pet knows some basic facts about animals," she began. "Like humans, they like to play and sleep and be well fed. They care for their young. They feel hunger, fear, pain, anger, pleasure, loyalty, and love."

The crowd became quiet as Dana continued. "Unlike us, animals don't kill for fun. They kill to survive. Do we have the right to end their lives for our own amusement?"

There was an immediate outburst of applause and jeers.

"Maggie was right," Bess said, next to Nancy. "The town is completely divided over this issue."

Dana spoke for a few more minutes. Nancy scanned the crowd. She had to agree with Maggie. There was a number of people here who had reason to threaten Dana. Could one of them have sabotaged the refuge? Nancy wondered.

"Put an end to hunting in Seven Rocks now!" Dana finished with her fist raised high. There was a mix of applause and angry calls as she left the stage. Then a burly man took her place. He began to talk about the delicate ecosystem of the Rockies.

Dana threaded her way through the crowd to Nancy and her friends.

"You were terrific," George said warmly.

Dana wiped her brow with exaggerated relief. "Thanks," she said. "I'm always so nervous when I have to talk to a crowd."

"Well, you convinced us," Bess assured her. "Did you find the bear?"

"Not yet," Dana said with a worried expression. "But we'll keep searching." She smiled at Nancy. "Your cub seems to be doing pretty well, though. We're going to take him out of the clinic and put him in one of the outside cages today."

"His leg is all right?" asked Nancy.

"It's getting there," Dana said. "It will probably take about three weeks for the bone to heal. Then we'll release him back into the woods."

"I'll make sure to come visit him before we return home," Nancy told her.

Dana smiled. "Look, I'd love to talk, but there's a meeting of the antihunting group right after the rally. I've got to get some things together for it."

Nancy nodded. "Sure. But I need to talk to you for a moment." She reached into her jacket pocket, and her fingers closed on the threatening note. "I want to show you something I found yesterday near the bear's pen." Without further explanation, she handed Dana the note.

Dana unfolded the paper, and her hazel eyes widened with shock. She looked up at Nancy. "What—"

She never finished her question. A tall, sandy-haired man walked up to her and snatched the paper from her hand. "I'll just bet you've been waiting to hand me one of these," he said.

"Lucas!" Dana said with obvious irritation. "Give that back. It's not a flier!"

Looking slightly apologetic, the man handed the paper back to Dana. "Never mind," he told her. "I got one in the mail today, thank you very much."

"You're very welcome," Dana said with exaggerated courtesy. "Lucas Vaughn, I'd like you to meet three friends of mine: Nancy Drew, Bess Marvin, and George Fayne."

Lucas nodded to the girls and gave them a bright smile. "A pleasure, I'm sure."

Nancy couldn't quite figure out what was going on between Dana and Lucas. They obviously enjoyed annoying each other. "Did you like my speech?" Dana asked him.

"It was the highlight of my week," he assured her.

"That's good," Dana said. "Because there will be more. Good day, Mr. Vaughn."

She turned away, but he grabbed her elbow and turned her back to face him. "Just what are you trying to do?" he said in a serious tone. "Put me out of business?"

"That would be a start," Dana said. She glared at Lucas Vaughn, and he released her arm. "Lucas makes his living by taking tourists out to shoot animals," she explained to the others.

"I run hunting expeditions that are completely legal," Lucas reminded her. "And you know I'm careful about which animals I take."

"Tell *them*," Dana said, gesturing to the crowd.

Lucas arched one blond eyebrow. "I would if I could get up there without being stoned." He sighed, and Nancy thought he looked a bit weary. "Dana, you and I have been arguing since the day you learned to talk. But I'm telling you, you're going too far this time."

"Just wait and see how much further I go," Dana said calmly.

"All right," Lucas said. He raised his hands in surrender. "Let's change the subject. Have you heard anything from Steve lately?"

"I got a letter this morning," Dana answered. "He says to tell you he'll be home for Christmas.

You have an appointment with him then on Castle Run."

Lucas grinned and tipped his hat. "Tell Steve I'll be there."

Bess looked mystified as she watched Lucas stride into the crowd. "What was that all about?" she asked.

Dana sighed. "Besides running one of the most successful hunting outfits in the Rockies, Lucas Vaughn happens to be my brother's best friend. He practically grew up in our house. Now Steve's in San Diego, but they always have a killer ski competition when Steve comes home for Christmas."

Dana was still holding the note that had been left near the bear's pen.

"Do you think Lucas wrote that note?" Nancy asked bluntly. "It sounds like he's got a good reason to be angry with you."

Dana shrugged. "Lucas and I have always gotten on each other's nerves. Steve says we were just born that way."

"Then he might have been the one who released the bear," George said.

"Lucas?" Dana sounded surprised, but she hesitated a moment before answering. "This may sound strange," she said, "but even though he kills them, Lucas has a lot of respect for animals. I can't imagine him releasing a wounded bear."

"Well, do you have any other ideas on who would?" Nancy asked.

Slowly, Dana unfolded the note again. She looked up at Nancy with a troubled gaze and shook her head.

"Will you get in touch with me if you think of anyone?"

Dana nodded. "I promise," she said solemnly. "If I think of any suspects, I'll call you tonight from Paws."

Nancy looked around at the clean kitchen with satisfaction. She, George, and Bess had cooked dinner for the Larsens, and the meal had been a success. Somehow, though, she'd wound up doing most of the dishes. Bess, she knew, was upstairs writing postcards. She wasn't sure where George was.

Maybe I'll write some postcards myself, Nancy thought. She knew that her father and her boyfriend, Ned Nickerson, who was attending college, would be eager to hear about her latest case. But what will I tell them? Nancy wondered. I'm still a long way from solving this one.

Nancy found George sitting cross-legged on the living room rug with the trail map spread out before her.

George pointed to Cloud Lake. "You know, we

41

never did make it to the lake," she said. "If it's warm tomorrow, maybe we ought to try it again."

"I guess," Nancy said.

"That's an enthusiastic response," George teased. "Don't tell me—you've got other things on your mind."

Nancy smiled. "It's just that I've got so little to go on in this case. Someone is sabotaging the refuge and threatening Dana, I assume. And she seems to trust my prime suspect—Lucas Vaughn."

"Sometimes trust is misplaced," George said.

"I know. That's what worries me." Nancy sat down beside George and peered at the map. "There must be about forty hiking trails here," she said. "I vote for exploring some different scenery. Let's see if we can find another one with a lake."

The two girls were still poring over the map when Maggie called out, "Nancy, there's a phone call for you. It's Dana."

George raised her eyebrows. "Maybe she's thought of some new suspects."

"Let's hope so," Nancy said. She picked up the phone and knew at once that Dana hadn't called to discuss suspects. Dana's voice was shaking. "Nancy, I just got back to the refuge. Someone's set fire to the feed shed!"

5

The Sign of the Cat

"I think you should leave the refuge at once," Nancy told Dana. "Whoever set that fire may still be on the grounds. Why don't you come down to Seven Rocks and spend the night here? I'm sure Cal and Maggie wouldn't mind."

Dana hesitated. "No," she said finally. "I'm not going to be scared off my own land. Besides, the fire's out and Jesse's here with me. I can ask him to sleep in one of the spare bedrooms. I'll be perfectly safe."

But what about Jesse? Nancy thought. Could he be trusted? "Dana, where was Jesse when the fire was set?"

"He was in his cottage, listening to music," Dana

43

answered. "He smelled smoke and got a fire extinguisher from the main house. We're just lucky he got there before it really caught. He was putting it out when I arrived."

"I've got an idea," Nancy said. "What if George and Bess and I come up there and spend the night with you? We could make popcorn and—"

"Thanks, but I'll be fine," Dana said. "Jesse and I checked the grounds. There's no one here except the animals, and they're all secure in their pens. I just thought you should know what happened. I'll be okay. Really. I guess I just got a little panicky."

Nancy ran an impatient hand through her hair. "It's too dark now, but I'd like to take a look at the feed shed. How about tomorrow?"

"That'd be fine," Dana said. She sounded much calmer than she had at the start of the conversation. "Don't worry," she told Nancy. "I'm sure everything will be all right."

"I certainly hope so," Nancy said, and hung up the phone.

"I'm beginning to think Bess had the right idea sleeping late," Nancy said breathlessly. It was just after seven in the morning, and she and George had decided to go for an early run.

"Me, too," George huffed.

"Maggie's book said it takes about two weeks for

44

the body to adjust to the change in elevation," Nancy said.

"Great," George said. "As soon as we adjust, it'll be time to leave."

"I think," Nancy said, taking in a deep breath, "that this might be easier if we didn't try to talk."

George grinned and gave her a thumbs-up sign.

By now the girls were already well out of town. Aspens and evergreens lined the road on either side of them. The morning air was cool and fragrant, and all was quiet except for the occasional chirp of a bird. Nancy settled into a smooth, even pace, enjoying the autumn colors.

Suddenly, Nancy heard a truck behind them accelerate quite loudly. She turned to see a battered blue pickup truck, with a gun rack, increasing its speed. Then the truck swerved abruptly, heading straight for them.

"George," Nancy screamed, "get off the road!"

Instinct took over, and Nancy dove for the side of the road. She landed hard on the steep bank of a hill and immediately began rolling downward.

With a thump, she came to a stop against a tree. Another thump told her that George had landed somewhere nearby. Nancy waited for the world to stop spinning and then slowly sat up. Her left knee and both elbows were scraped but nothing else hurt.

George sat a short distance away, holding her left ankle. She looked over at Nancy. "Are you okay?" she called.

"I'm fine," Nancy replied. "But *you're* not, are you?"

"Well, I don't think it's anything serious," George reported. "My ankle's starting to swell, but I can move my foot. It's probably just a sprain."

Nancy got up and began searching the ground for something that would serve as a walking stick. "Don't worry," she told her friend. "We'll get you out of here." She found a thick branch about four feet high and gave it to George. "Do you think you could stand if you use this for support?"

"No problem," George said with a trace of her usual smile. She got to her feet slowly and began to hobble up the embankment.

"Are you in a lot of pain?" Nancy asked.

George winced. "Only when I do something dumb like put weight on my foot."

Finally, they reached the road. "We must be about three miles from Seven Rocks," George said, breathing hard. "At this rate we'll make it back by nightfall."

"Take your time," Nancy said patiently. "We can stop and rest whenever you need to." But despite her calm tone, Nancy was worried. She was convinced that the blue pickup running them off the

46

road hadn't been an accident. Someone knew she was on the case and wanted her off. What if that someone came back?

They hadn't gone more than a half mile when a shiny white pickup slowed to a stop beside them. Lucas Vaughn leaned out the window.

"Mornin', ladies," he said, giving them a friendly smile and looking down at George's foot. "Looks like you could use a ride."

"Could we ever!" Nancy told him, and she and George climbed in the truck.

"How did you manage to do that?" Lucas asked, shifting the truck into first.

Lucas frowned as George told him the story. "A battered blue pickup with a gun rack," he mused. "Did either of you catch the license plate number?"

George shook his head. "It happened too fast."

"Crazy drivers," Lucas said. "Well, don't worry. I'll get you back to town, and Maggie will take good care of you. That woman can handle anything."

Nancy studied Lucas Vaughn's handsome profile. He seemed genuinely concerned about George. Somehow Nancy couldn't believe he'd had anything to do with running them off the road. But was Lucas the one sabotaging the refuge? She decided to take a direct approach. "Dana called us last night," she began.

"Lucky you," Lucas said.

Nancy ignored his comment. "Someone set fire to the feed shed up at Paws yesterday," she went on.

Lucas shrugged. "Maybe Miss Walsh is finally getting what's coming to her."

"It sounds almost like you approve," George said.

"You can be sure I had nothing to do with it. I run a business," he told them. "I don't have time for tricks like that. Why don't you check out that weird McKay kid who works with her?"

"I intend to," Nancy assured him as they passed a sign welcoming them to Seven Rocks. "Why do you think Jesse is weird?"

"Why?" Lucas gave her a look of disbelief. "A year ago, I told Dana that boy was trouble. There's just something about him that doesn't sit right. Of course, Dana, being the stubborn mule that she is, hired him, anyway." He stopped for a red light, and his voice became softer. "I'm sorry, but your friend Dana is making things very difficult for me. I'm about out of patience with her."

Nancy and George exchanged questioning looks. Lucas was every bit as hard to figure out as Jesse was. Dana was clearly a thorn in his side, yet he seemed oddly protective of her. But no one had more reason to try and stop Dana than Lucas. Maybe Lucas was trying to throw suspicion on Jesse by telling her he was trouble.

Nancy knew she had to find out more about Lucas Vaughn, but how? Then he surprised her by saying quite cheerfully, "I've decided it's time to change my tactics. I'm going to give hunters some good publicity for a change. Tomorrow, Vaughn Outfitters is holding an open house. We'll be giving tracking, archery, and marksmanship demonstrations, along with talks on stalking some of the bigger game animals."

Nancy spoke up quickly. "If it's all right, I'd like to come."

Both George and Lucas looked at her in surprise. "Do you hunt?" he asked.

"Not animals. Only criminals," Nancy answered as he pulled up in front of the Larsen house.

George lay on the Larsens' living room couch, propped up on an assortment of flowered pillows. Munro sat purring on her stomach. Nancy watched worriedly as Dr. Yan gently removed an ice pack and examined George's injured ankle.

"Well," the doctor said at last. "You do have a mild sprain. Your ankle should be fine in a day or so if you stay off it."

"She will," Maggie promised, entering the room with another fresh ice pack.

Dr. Yan smiled and reached for his bag. "I can see I'm leaving you in excellent hands."

The doctor had no sooner left than the doorbell rang again. "Do you think that's Bess?" George asked. "Where is she, anyway?"

"I forgot to tell you. Bess went into town to do some shopping," Maggie said, going to the door. "This must be the police. I called the station after I called the doctor." She opened the door to admit a trim woman with short blond hair and very green eyes.

"Nancy Drew, George Fayne," Maggie said, "I'd like you to meet Sergeant Linda Baker."

Sergeant Baker smiled at the girls and sat down in the chair nearest George. "So," she began, "Maggie tells me you were the victims of an attempted hit-and-run this morning."

"It's possible whoever was driving that truck didn't really want to hit us," Nancy said thoughtfully. "It might have been more of a warning."

"You mean, to stay off the case?" George asked.

Sergeant Baker raised her eyebrows. "The case?"

"Sergeant Baker," Nancy said, "do you know what's been going on up at Paws?"

"I know what kind of trouble Dana's been stirring up in town," Sergeant Baker replied. "But Paws is twenty miles away. It's out of my jurisdiction, I'm afraid."

Nancy gave a detailed report of being run off the

road, then she described Dana's troubles. "I'm not sure whether what happened to us this morning is connected," she finished. "I never rule out possibilities like that, though."

"Neither do I," the sergeant said. "Maybe I'll pay a visit to Paws."

"What about the truck?" George asked. "Can you track down one that fits the description?"

Sergeant Baker shook her head doubtfully. "Out here, blue pickups with gun racks are about as common as pine trees. But we'll do a computer check and see what we come up with."

"The truck that Lucas Vaughn was driving was white," Nancy said. "Maybe the blue one belongs to someone who works for him."

"I'll check," Sergeant Baker said. "But truthfully, Nancy, I can't imagine Lucas being our culprit. Or one of his men, for that matter. Lucas is a careful man with a very successful business. It'd be unlikely that he would risk something illegal."

The sergeant looked at George's ankle and frowned. "Normally, Seven Rocks is a peaceful little town," she said, "but tensions are running high now. I want the two of you to be extremely careful and keep one fact in mind. This morning someone may have tried to kill you."

When Sergeant Baker left, Nancy turned to

George and said, "Would you mind terribly if I left you for a little while? Bess should be back from town soon."

"You want to go up to Paws, right?"

"I have to," Nancy said. "I want to take a look at that feed shed before any clues vanish."

"Nancy," Maggie broke in, "didn't you hear what Sergeant Baker just said?"

"Paws is out of Sergeant Baker's jurisdiction," Nancy replied. "That means it's up to me to help Dana."

"What would your father say if he knew you were in danger?" Maggie asked.

"He'd probably tell me to be careful, but he wouldn't stop me from investigating," Nancy answered honestly. "Dad got used to my being a detective a long time ago."

Maggie sighed. "I suppose you're right," she said. "But please be very careful."

"Don't worry. I will," Nancy said, heading toward the door.

A half hour later, Nancy stopped the car in front of the main house at the Paws compound. She hoped that it would be Dana, and not Jesse, who greeted her.

Her wish was answered as Dana came out of the

house, looking hot and exhausted. Her face brightened when she saw Nancy. "I was just about to take a break," she said. "Jesse and I have spent all morning building a new shed and moving in the feed that wasn't destroyed. Want to join me for a lemonade?"

"That'd be great," Nancy said.

She and Dana settled themselves on the stone porch of the old mansion with two glasses and a large pitcher of lemonade beside them. "Dana," Nancy began, "can you tell me exactly what happened last night?"

"I got back up here at about eight," Dana said. "I was really tired from the rally and meetings. That's why, I guess, I didn't notice the smell of smoke until I was nearly in the house." She stopped for a moment, taking a sip of her drink. "When I ran toward the animal compounds, I could hear that the animals were hysterical. The coyote was barking, the cougar was yowling; even the badger was making these high-pitched screaming noises. By the time I got to the small-animal compound, I was terrified. I had no idea what I'd find."

"What exactly did you see?" Nancy prompted.

"Well, as I told you, the feed shed was on fire—or smoldering. It hadn't really caught. Luckily, Jesse had given the mule deer a bath yesterday

53

morning. He managed to get everything soaked, so the wood was still damp. Anyway, I found Jesse spraying foam all over the place with a fire extinguisher."

"Did Jesse say how the fire started?" Nancy asked.

"No," Dana replied. "He told me that he was in the cottage listening to a tape when he smelled the smoke. And he didn't see anyone." She sighed. "You think Jesse had something to do with it, don't you?"

"I don't know," Nancy told her truthfully. "But I want to find out. There isn't any way the fire could have started on its own, is there? I mean, flammable rags or something?"

"No," Dana said. "Nothing like that."

"Where is Jesse now?"

"Where he usually is. With the mountain lion."

Nancy stood up. "I'd like to ask him a few questions. Then I'll have a look at the feed shed."

Dana nodded. "We can visit your cub on the way."

Dana led Nancy through the small-animal compound and stopped in front of a roomy cage where the little mountain lion stood in a corner, its rear leg splinted. It regarded Nancy solemnly and gave two tiny cries.

"Are you feeling better?" Nancy asked it.

"It ate a mouse this morning," Dana informed her. "It's going to be fine."

They found Jesse in the large-animal compound. He was standing near the mountain lion's cage, his attention focused on the big cat. Nancy stepped into the clearing and stopped. The cat had seen them and was hissing a furious warning. Jesse whirled in alarm, then relaxed as he saw Dana and Nancy.

After her first bewildering meeting with Jesse, Nancy decided to approach Jesse with caution. Maybe the way to get him to open up was to talk about animals. "She's magnificent," Nancy said, nodding toward the mountain lion.

"Yeah," the boy agreed.

"Do you think she's starting to trust you?" Nancy asked.

"I hope not," he answered. "If she's going to survive, she'd better regard all humans as her enemies. I'm not trying to befriend her. I just can't help watching her."

The mountain lion was pacing now, giving low, nervous growls each time it reached one end of the pen.

"What happened to its side?" Nancy asked.

"Got in a fight with another animal," the boy answered.

Nancy sighed. Jesse wasn't becoming any friendlier, but she wasn't ready to give up. "Jesse," Nancy said carefully, "can you tell me what happened last night when you found the feed shed on fire?"

Instantly, Jesse's face became blank. "No."

"Jesse, please," Dana said. "We're trying to find out who's been sabotaging the refuge."

Jesse gave her an unreadable look. "I don't like nosy strangers," he said. Then he turned and walked toward the cottage.

"I'm sorry," Dana said to Nancy. "It's just that . . . Jesse doesn't trust many people."

"Dana, how much do you know about Jesse?" Nancy asked.

Dana hooked her thumbs in her pockets and began to walk back toward the small-animal compound. "Jesse showed up here about a year ago, looking for work," she said. "He was pretty vague about where he came from. Somewhere in southern Colorado, I think. He said he'd grown up on a ranch and knew animals. And he does." Dana sighed. "Jesse and I get along because we're both crazy about animals. We're not exactly what you'd call close, though. Sometimes I think that Jesse and that mountain lion are a lot alike. Neither of them trusts anyone. And they've both got something wild in them."

"Well," Nancy pressed, "is there anything about Jesse that would give you cause for suspicion?"

Dana shook her head. "I've never met a better worker," she answered. "I trust Jesse McKay completely. I'm sure he's had nothing to do with these incidents. Now, if you'll excuse me, I want to look again for that bear while it's still daylight. I'll be in touch with you. And thanks for your help."

Nancy walked to the feed shed and found it to be just as Dana had described it. The small wooden structure was partially burned, and the smell of charred wood lingered in the air. Nancy examined the site carefully. She chided herself for not asking Dana to leave it untouched until she'd had a chance to look at it.

Picking up a large stick, Nancy began to poke through the burned debris. She sifted through sticks, bits of wood, the remains of a burlap feed sack, and suddenly her eyes lighted on a piece of an envelope.

Her heart pounding, Nancy knelt and picked up the envelope. Most of it had been torn off, and whatever message had been inside was gone. But Nancy could see that the envelope was addressed to Jesse. And in the corner was the sign of the cat.

6

A Trap

Nancy stood staring at the drawing of the cat on the torn envelope. Whoever was sabotaging Paws wasn't after Dana—he or she was after Jesse McKay.

But what if the culprit was working *with* Jesse? The envelope might have been a message to him. That theory was shaky, Nancy realized. There was no good reason for Jesse to endanger either Dana or the refuge. The one thing she knew for sure about Jesse was that he genuinely cared about animals. So why would he be mixed up in anything that would harm them?

Nancy shook her head and slipped what remained of the envelope into her jacket pocket. She was no closer to solving this mystery than she'd been that morning. But she had proof that Jesse and the sign of the cat were connected.

Now what? she asked herself. She was tempted to confront Jesse with the envelope, but confronting Jesse on anything didn't seem to work very well.

Lost in thought, Nancy made her way back to her car. She stopped as she rounded the corner of the main house. There was a rustling sound in the woods to the side of the house. It could be the wind or a rabbit. Or even her imagination.

Then there was another sound that definitely was not in her mind—the sound of a car door slamming. At the very end of the estate's drive, Nancy saw a battered blue pickup. It was swinging out of a thicket, where it had been concealed. Before she even reached her car, the blue truck tore out of the drive.

As quickly as she could, Nancy got into her car and started after the truck. Flooring the gas pedal, she raced along the estate road. She reached the main road just in time to see the blue pickup heading down the mountain.

What a place for a chase, Nancy thought as she followed the truck. The mountain road was one hairpin turn after another.

Ahead, Nancy heard the tires of the blue pickup screeching. I'll just have to risk it, Nancy told herself.

Rounding a curve, she picked up speed. The yellow rental car swerved to the side, skidding dangerously close to the edge of the mountain. For a moment, Nancy was sure that the car was out of control, but with her quick reflexes she steered it back onto the road. Nancy wished she had her own blue sports car, which handled much better than the rental.

Nancy continued to pursue the truck, determined to find out who drove it. But she couldn't go much faster than thirty miles an hour and still take the turns safely. By the time she was halfway down the mountain, Nancy knew she'd lost the blue pickup.

It was almost dark when Nancy returned to Seven Rocks. As she got out of her car, she met Maggie and Cal coming down the walk. Cal was dressed up, wearing a light tan jacket over darker pants. Maggie looked elegant in a simple lavender dress.

"Where are you two going?" Nancy teased, glad for a distraction from her case. "This looks like a formal date."

Maggie gave her husband's outfit a look of mild disapproval. "Yes," she said. "This is about as formal as Cal gets."

Cal pretended to be offended. "We are going to

the opera," he said in a mock-British accent. "My wife has decided I'm in need of culture."

"What?" Maggie demanded indignantly. "You're the one who insisted we get tickets!"

Cal kissed her, laughing. "We'll sort it out in the car." He turned to Nancy. "You'll find George and Bess inside."

"How is George?" Nancy asked.

"The swelling in her ankle is down," Maggie answered. "Bess is already threatening to tie her to the couch if she doesn't take it easy." Maggie smiled. "I believe Bess already has your evening organized. Have fun!"

Nancy soon discovered that Bess indeed had everything planned. "We need a quiet night," she said, looking meaningfully at George.

"I've already had a quiet afternoon," said George.

"Good." Nancy sat down on the couch beside her friend. "Are you feeling better?"

"I'd feel a lot better if Nurse Bess would let me get up," George complained.

Nancy's blue eyes sparkled with amusement. "I'm glad you're well enough to give us a hard time, but don't forget what Dr. Yan said."

"Exactly," Bess chimed in. "Come on, George, we'll have fun. I've made popcorn and rented a movie." She held up a box. "I even found Maggie's Scrabble game just in case we all hate the movie."

"What did you rent?" Nancy asked.

Bess looked a little sheepish. "Well, I could only get my fifth choice. Seven Rocks only has one video store. I wound up with an old western."

Nancy laughed. "Turn it on, pardner. I could use some exciting entertainment."

"You're not going to tell us what happened up at Paws?" George asked.

"After the movie," Nancy promised.

Bess brought in the popcorn, and the three girls curled up in front of the TV. Nancy allowed herself to be drawn into the western. It was the story of two brothers—one was a sheriff, and the other a cattle rustler. Of course, the sheriff wound up trying to arrest the cattle rustler. The cattle rustler was always doing things like stealing the sheriff's girlfriend and hiding in a horse trough when his pursuers got too close.

Munro settled himself beside Nancy. She scratched him absently behind the ears, and he purred contentedly. Nancy thought of Dana's speech. Here was an animal who showed trust, affection, intelligence, and a bit of temper if rubbed the wrong way.

"This is great!" Bess said enthusiastically as the cattle rustler engaged in a long kiss with the woman who ran the saloon. "I'd be in love with the cattle rustler, too. He's so much more exciting."

Nancy's attention went back to the TV. "He's definitely got more style," she agreed.

"Mmmm," George said. "I'm with you."

Nancy yawned, content to lose herself in the movie. Sometime after the cattle rustler held up a train and stole an emerald ring for his lady, she fell asleep.

She awoke with a start to hear Maggie shouting, "Cal, no! Don't move!"

"What's going on?" Nancy asked sleepily.

Bess started toward the door. Nancy was beside her instantly, turning on the porch light and opening the front door.

"No!" Maggie and Cal shouted at the same time. "Don't come out!"

"Oh!" Nancy and Bess said together. On the veranda, centered right in front of the door, were the gleaming metal jaws of an open steel trap.

"My heavens," said Maggie, recovering her composure. "Who would put such a thing here? Cal was ahead of me and almost walked right into it."

"Everyone stay where you are for a moment," Cal said. "I'll be right back." He disappeared around the side of the house and returned a few minutes later with a rake. Holding the rake upside down, Cal used the thick wooden handle to spring the

63

trap. The trap clamped shut, neatly snapping the rake in two.

"Oooh," Bess shuddered. "Thank goodness no one got caught in that."

"Is it a bear trap?" Nancy asked.

"That's right," Cal said briskly. "You don't see many of these around anymore. I'm not even sure it's still legal to use them."

"I'm calling the police," Maggie said, sweeping past them and into the house.

Nancy knelt beside the trap, wondering if the police would be able to take prints from it. "Oh, no," she murmured.

"What is it?" asked Bess.

Nancy pointed to the white wooden flooring. In charcoal, someone had drawn the sign of the cat.

An hour later, Sergeant Baker was once again in the Larsens' living room, taking notes. She had already dusted the trap for prints, but it was clean. Whoever left the trap had been extremely careful.

Nancy suddenly remembered Sergeant Baker's words about Lucas Vaughn: "He's a careful man."

"Sergeant Baker," Nancy said, "the trap is something hunters use. Do you think it could be a message from Lucas?"

Cal snorted. "Lucas is too smart to do something that obvious. Besides, if Lucas wanted to get some-

64

one, he wouldn't be sending symbolic messages. He'd come straight out and say what he meant. He wouldn't endanger other people while he was going about it, either."

"I'm afraid I have to agree," Sergeant Baker said.

"Speaking of messages," Nancy said, "I have something." She took out the envelope she'd found at Paws.

"It's the same cat, all right," Sergeant Baker said. "Now I'm almost certain that what happened on the road this morning was no accident. Whoever is harassing Dana—and maybe Jesse—is sending *you* messages, too."

"Nancy, I don't like this," Cal said, looking concerned. "I know you get involved in this sort of thing all the time, but that trap could have hurt any one of us. Five people were in danger tonight."

"I know," Nancy said. "And I'm sorry—"

"No one said it was your fault," Maggie interrupted.

"Certainly not," Cal said. "And I'm not asking you to drop the case. I just don't want to see anyone get hurt."

"I understand," Nancy said quietly. "I don't want anyone to get hurt, either." She looked around the room at her friends and felt more torn than ever. She cared about all of these people. George had already gotten hurt, and Cal and Maggie were upset. How much more could any of them take before she solved the case? But how could she abandon Dana when she was clearly in danger?

Sergeant Baker stood up. "I'd better go," she said. "And I'll take that bear trap with me."

"You're welcome to it," Cal muttered.

The police officer smiled at him. "Tell me," she said, "since your information is almost always better than ours, has there been any news on those escaped convicts?"

"What?" Cal asked distractedly. "Oh, yes. A wire came in before I left this afternoon. All but two of them were recaptured. They were caught heading south toward New Mexico, I believe."

Sergeant Baker chuckled. "Actually, that's the same thing we heard. For once our networks must be working properly." She turned toward the others. "Try and get some rest, all of you. I'll have my people keep an eye on the house."

Bess and Cal helped George up the stairs, but Nancy followed Sergeant Baker out onto the porch. "Did you go up to the refuge?" Nancy asked.

"Early this evening. The truth is, you found more than I did." Sergeant Baker leaned against the porch railing and shook her head ruefully. "If you ever want a career in police work, you'll have my recommendation."

"Thanks," Nancy said, smiling. "You talked to Dana and Jesse then?"

Sergeant Baker nodded.

"What did you think of Jesse?"

The police officer answered immediately. "Exactly what I thought when he first showed up in Seven Rocks last year: Jesse McKay is hiding something."

7

Open House

The next morning Nancy, George, and Bess sat at the kitchen table, finishing breakfast. Both Cal and Maggie had already gone out. The three friends were trying to decide what they were going to do that day.

"Just a little hike," George insisted. "The swelling's almost completely gone. My ankle feels fine."

"I'm glad you're better," Bess said. "But I still don't think you should go hiking so soon."

Nancy finished the last of her orange juice. "She's right, George. Besides, I have a better idea. Let's go to Lucas Vaughn's open house."

"But all those guns being shot . . ." Bess complained.

George put her head down in her hands and

mumbled, "Some people have strange ideas about how to have fun." The morning sunlight played on her short brown hair, bringing out its reddish highlights.

"Oh, George," Bess said. "We should put henna in your hair. You'll make a gorgeous redhead!"

"Oh, that's just what I want to do today," George complained good-naturedly. "Put henna in my hair. Why didn't I think of that?"

"Cut it out, you two," Nancy said, laughing. "Look, we don't have to stay long, but I need more information on Lucas Vaughn. The open house is the perfect opportunity to get it."

"Count me in," said George. "It's got to be better than henna."

"Oh, okay," Bess said reluctantly. She grinned at her cousin. "We'll do your hair another time."

After doing the breakfast dishes, the girls got in the car and consulted their map. Nancy had no trouble finding her way to Lucas Vaughn's. Lucas had posted signs advertising the open house all along the road that led to his land.

"We're here," George said. Ahead of them, to the left, was a wooden sign announcing Vaughn Outfitters. On top of the sign was the mounted head of a bighorn sheep.

"I knew this would be too much for me," Bess said from the backseat, looking at the sheep's head.

69

Nancy felt her hands tighten on the steering wheel. "We won't stay long," she said again, turning into the drive. Following more signs, they took a dirt road uphill, past a large A-frame building. The sound of gunshots filled the air.

"Maybe I'll stay in the car," Bess said.

"Lucas said there would be a marksmanship demonstration," George told her cousin. "That means they're shooting clay pigeons."

Nancy pulled into a parking area on the top of the hill, and the three girls followed more signs to a grassy clearing. There they found the marksmanship exhibition.

They joined a crowd of visitors and watched as a man wearing a Vaughn T-shirt and holding a shotgun yelled, "Pull!" A split second later, two clay disks spun into the air. The man shouldered his gun and fired twice. Both disks shattered.

"Pull!" the man cried again. This time he missed the second disk. He finished to applause from the crowd and was given a score.

Next Lucas Vaughn stepped up and took the man's place. Lucas was wearing jeans, western boots, and a blue denim shirt. Nancy thought he looked completely relaxed. He held the shotgun effortlessly, as if it were a part of his body. Then he shot twenty rounds without missing a single disk.

He grinned at the applause that followed and

waved it down. "We have an archery demonstration next," he announced. "This way, please. . . ."

Nancy and her friends followed the crowd to an area where six large bull's-eye targets had been set up. One by one, Lucas and five other men lined up a distance from the targets. Each had a heavy hunting bow and a quiver of arrows. All of the men were skilled, but only Lucas sent ten arrows flying straight to the heart of the target.

George watched, fascinated. Nancy knew George had won a few archery contests herself. "How would you rate Lucas?" she asked.

George thought for a moment. "Lucas Vaughn could be an extremely dangerous man if he wanted to be," she said.

"He already is if you're an animal," Bess observed.

One of Lucas's men announced a tracking demonstration. As the crowd began to move again, Lucas spotted the three girls. He came over to them at once.

"I didn't really think you'd show," he said, sounding pleased that they had. His blue eyes went to George. "How's the ankle?"

"Much better. The doctor said it was probably just a mild sprain."

Lucas looked doubtful. "Even so, you probably shouldn't be standing on it so much. Look, I've got

71

to go down to the office for a few minutes. Why don't you three come along?" His eyes lit on Nancy with a teasing challenge. "Unless, of course, you're in need of a tracking lesson?"

"I think I can skip the tracking class," Nancy said, laughing. She was curious about what she might find in Lucas's office. "Come on, George. It couldn't hurt to rest for a while."

George looked slightly reluctant but didn't argue. The three girls followed Lucas down the hill.

Lucas opened the door to the A-frame. The entire first floor was apparently his office. A gun rack stood in one corner beneath a large topographic map. Mounted hunting trophies hung on every wall. Nancy swallowed hard as she looked at the heads of a five-point buck, a bear, an elk, another bighorn sheep, and directly behind Lucas's desk, a mountain lion.

Bess jumped when she brushed against a stuffed bear standing near the door.

Lucas took mugs from a shelf beside an automatic coffee machine. "Make yourselves comfortable, ladies," he said, indicating a leather couch and several wooden chairs. "Can I offer you some coffee?"

Bess and George declined and sat on the couch. Nancy looked around for a bear trap that was similar to the one that had been left on the Larsens' porch but didn't see anything like it.

"I'll take a cup of coffee, thank you," Nancy said, and then added casually, "Did you catch any of these animals with traps?"

Lucas fixed two mugs of coffee. "I've never used a trap in my life," he replied calmly. "I don't like to see an animal suffer."

Nancy took the mug of coffee from Lucas and walked slowly around the room, looking for any sign that would connect Lucas with the incidents of the past few days. One thing was clear: His business was every bit as successful as Sergeant Baker had said. The office was expensively furnished, and a thick Oriental rug covered the polished wood floor. Upstairs, through the balcony railing, Nancy could see spacious living quarters.

Her eyes slid to Lucas's desk. She noticed what looked like a handwritten letter. At the bottom in straight, even script, Lucas had signed his name. His handwriting didn't look anything like the Cat's.

The phone rang before Nancy could frame her next question. "Excuse me," Lucas said, picking up the receiver. At first he listened. Then his good-humored expression suddenly went dark. "Now, hold on," he broke in, but the caller interrupted. Lucas sat back, obviously trying to hold on to his

73

patience. "Yes, you'll get your refund!" he snapped finally, and hung up the phone.

He gave Nancy a brief, angry glance. "It's time I had a talk with your friend," he said, punching in a number quickly. There was a second's pause while the call was picked up. Then Lucas spoke in a dangerously quiet voice. "I'm not playing with you now, Dana. I've just had my seventh cancellation this week, thanks to that campaign of yours. You keep pushing it, and you and I are going to be at war." He hung up without giving Dana a chance to reply.

George gave Nancy a look that seemed to say, "This guy means business."

Just then one of Lucas's men entered the office. "Got a few people who want a price on a five-day trip," he told Lucas. "Think you could talk to them?"

"I'll be right there," Lucas said. He nodded to George, the anger gone from his voice. "Does your ankle feel better after the rest?"

"I'm fine," said George, standing up.

"After you," he said to the girls, giving them a gallant half-bow.

Nancy, George, and Bess preceded Lucas out of the A-frame, and Lucas stayed behind to talk to the group waiting for him. "I've never met anyone else

I've liked *and* disliked at the same time," George said, starting up the hill.

"I know what you mean," Nancy agreed. Her mind was going over what she'd seen in the office. Lucas seemed to be a nice man until he was confronted with Dana's antihunting campaign. "Did you notice anything in there that would link Lucas to the sign of the cat?" Nancy asked George.

George shrugged. "Maybe that poor cougar mounted over his desk?"

"I don't think that's enough," Nancy said. "It was just one more trophy. I have a feeling whoever has been leaving those drawings identifies with the cat somehow. It seems almost as if it's his signature. And I didn't see anything around Lucas's office that suggested that." She grinned. "I even looked at a letter he'd written that was on his desk."

"Don't forget we heard him threaten Dana," George said.

"I know. And I keep thinking about what Cal said about Lucas. That he's very straightforward. And he was. When he got mad at Dana, he called her and told her so. With us sitting right there," Nancy added. "Would he threaten her that openly if he's the one who's been sabotaging Paws all along? He acts like he has nothing to hide."

Nancy stopped walking as they reached the parking area. "Maybe we ought to have a look for that blue pickup." Nancy, Bess, and George circled the lot, checking thoroughly, but the blue pickup was nowhere in sight.

"Where did Bess go?" George asked, joining Nancy on one side of the lot. "Do you think she went to the tracking class?"

Nancy smiled at the idea. "Maybe *we* should. I didn't get much information from Lucas's office."

Bess was indeed trailing along with the tracking group, which had been making its way alongside the parking lot. She saw Nancy and George and waved them over.

"So have you learned how to stalk the wild cottontail rabbit?" George joked.

"Shhh!" Bess said in a whisper. "Just stay close to me and listen."

Beside Bess a group of men were talking in low voices. "We could hold our own rally," one of them said.

"Or we could just put a stop to Dana Walsh," said a second.

"I hear she's been having troubles up at the refuge," added a third.

"Not nearly enough, if you ask me," said the second man. "After that rally yesterday, I lost three guests at the inn. One says he'll stay for Gaslight Night, but he canceled the rest of a two-week reservation. I'm tired of losing money just because that woman is a bleeding heart for every critter with fur or feathers."

"It's not just Dana," the first man reminded him. "She's got a lot of supporters in town."

"Well, none of them stirred up trouble before she started her campaign," said the second. "And we're going to have to do something about it."

The men broke apart as the tracking demonstration ended, and Lucas announced a list of other activities.

"That didn't exactly narrow down our list of suspects," George said with a sigh.

"No," Nancy admitted. "I'm beginning to wonder just how many people want to put a stop to Dana Walsh."

8

Gaslight Night

Wearing jeans and a light blue T-shirt, Nancy sat on the Larsens' veranda, letting the morning sun dry her hair. She'd just gone for a run and showered. And ever since she'd woken up, she'd been turning the case over and over in her mind.

Yesterday, after returning from Vaughn's, she and Bess and George had joined Maggie for a lazy afternoon swim at Angel Lake. Though Nancy had asked her about the other people in town determined to stop Dana, Maggie had not been able to give her any solid leads. When Nancy called Dana later that day, she learned that nothing new had happened at the refuge.

"Maggie's got fresh-baked muffins in the kitch-

78

en," Bess announced. She sailed out the porch door, a fat cranberry muffin in one hand. "You know," she said, sitting down next to Nancy, "I think I could get used to this spa life."

George followed her, smiling. "You do seem to be adapting pretty well." She gave Nancy a concerned look. "Still thinking about the case?"

"I can't help feeling there's something I'm missing," Nancy admitted. "I know Lucas has a solid reason to go after Dana, and that he threatened her. But somehow I don't think he's the one who's responsible for the sabotage. And he wasn't the person who ran us off the road."

"How about those men yesterday?" Bess asked.

Nancy shrugged. "It sounded like they *wanted* to do something, but they hadn't actually gotten around to it yet."

"Then we're back to Jesse," George said.

"Except that Jesse doesn't have a good motive," Nancy pointed out. "Besides, that envelope was addressed to him. For all we know, *he's* the one being threatened, not Dana."

Bess giggled and offered Nancy a piece of her muffin. "Blame it on Phineas Josiah Armbruster."

"That's not a bad idea," Nancy said slowly.

George raised a skeptical eyebrow. "Blaming a ghost?"

79

"Not exactly," Nancy said. "But I'm going to ask Cal if there have been any more sightings at the Midnight Mine. I also want to ask him if he's gotten any reports on a blue pickup. Maybe the sabotage at Paws was committed by someone we don't know about at all. Sort of a phantom suspect."

The door to the porch swung open, and Maggie stepped onto the veranda. She was carrying a vase filled with delicate ivory-colored orchids. She set it on a small wicker end table. "When I married Cal, he promised me that even if we didn't always have food on the table, I would have fresh flowers every day. That man keeps his promises. He sent so many of these today, I have enough for four vases."

"What a romantic," Bess sighed.

"And a spendthrift," Maggie said with a laugh. "But speaking of romantic, what have you three done to get ready for Gaslight Night? It's only hours away."

Earlier that week Maggie had explained that once a year Seven Rocks celebrated Gaslight Night, a return to the Victorian era, which was when the main part of the town had been built. The streets would be closed to all vehicles that weren't horse-drawn, and there would be free performances throughout the town—plays and songs depicting the early days of Seven Rocks' history. Best of all, everyone in town would be decked out in full Victorian dress.

"Nothing," Nancy and George answered at once.

"I thought so," said Bess triumphantly. "Luckily, while you two were off jogging and getting run off the road by that horrible blue truck, I was scouting the local stores. There's a wonderful little boutique called Nellie's that's a combination vintage clothing store and costume rental. I've picked out the perfect dresses for all of us."

George winced, but before she could protest, Maggie said, "Nellie's is exactly what I was going to suggest. You'd better hurry, though, or all the best dresses will be rented."

Half an hour later, the girls set out for Nellie's. Nancy was looking forward to tonight's celebration. Gaslight Night sounded like fun. It also sounded as if everyone in Seven Rocks would be there. Maybe she'd get a little closer to solving the case.

"Isn't this place wonderful?" Bess asked as they came to a storefront with an ornate sign in the window that read Nellie's Apparel and Sundries.

"Sundries?" George whispered.

"Odds and ends," Bess translated.

Nancy stepped into the boutique. It was furnished like a Victorian parlor, and everything seemed dark and rich and ornate. There were great oval mirrors in gilded frames on the walls, chairs covered in deep green velvet, and lamps with crystal prisms hanging from their glass shades. Four huge open wardrobes displayed Nellie's selection of antique dresses. A steamer trunk overflowed with lace petticoats and camisoles. The "dressing room" was a large area set off behind two heavy, painted wooden screens.

"The dresses I picked out for us are still here," said Bess with relief. "And they're all rentals."

Almost before Nancy knew what was happening, Bess had taken the dresses from the wardrobes and whisked her two friends behind the screens.

"Now," Bess said with great authority, "I thought this one would be perfect for George." She held up a simply cut gown of lilac tulle.

George rolled her eyes.

"Try it on and see how it looks," Nancy urged.

George reluctantly reached for the dress while Bess held up a confection of pink satin ruffles for herself.

"And for Nancy—" Bess dramatically flourished the third dress.

Nancy's face lit up when she saw the lovely ivory gown of silk and lace. If she'd had to design a dream dress, she couldn't have done better. "Oh, Bess, you know what I like," she said. "I hope it fits."

A few moments later, all three girls stood in front of the mirror. "Bess, you really have an eye for clothing," Nancy marveled. "These are perfect. George's looks like it was made for her."

"I had no idea we could be so elegant," George said, laughing.

"But of course, my dear," Bess trilled with a fake upper-class accent. "Let us return to the Larsen estate and prepare ourselves for this evening's festivities."

Maggie was delighted with the girls' choices. "All you need now are the finishing touches," she said. "And for that I suggest Larsen's Sundries."

Maggie led the way to the attic. There she opened an old trunk filled with things she'd inherited from her great-grandmother: stiff, starched petticoats, rhinestone tiaras, beaded handbags, long dress gloves, lace parasols and fans, and combs made of silver and shell. There was even a corset.

"Oh, could I wear that?" Bess asked. "I've always wanted a tiny waist."

"Corsets aren't very comfortable," Maggie said doubtfully. "But you're welcome to it."

Bess had her heart set on the corset. She gathered it up along with a few other "sundries," and the girls returned to their room to dress.

Getting into the antique dresses wasn't easy. All three had dozens of tiny buttons that fastened up the back.

"How did any woman ever close her own dress?" George wondered.

"She didn't," Bess answered, sliding the corset over her head. "That's what husbands and servants were for. Will you help me tighten my corset?"

Nancy and George nearly collapsed with laughter as they tried to lace Bess into the impossible garment.

"Aren't you having enough trouble breathing in this altitude?" asked an unbelieving George.

"It's no wonder women were always fainting back then," Nancy agreed. "Victorian styles may be gorgeous, but I'd take jeans any day rather than wear one of these things."

Bess began to pin her blond curls on top of her head. "I think corsets are very flattering," she said with a sniff.

"Insane," George said.

All of the girls had borrowed petticoats that made the long skirts of their dresses seem to float just above the ground. Bess topped her outfit off with long white gloves, a lace fan, and a rhinestone tiara. "Why not go all the way?" she asked with a giggle. Maggie insisted on lending George amethyst earrings that matched her dress perfectly. Nancy pinned up her hair with two silver combs, and at the last moment Maggie tucked in one of the ivory orchids.

"Ah," Cal said, watching the three girls descend the staircase with unusual dignity. "What a sight to behold."

Maggie and Cal were quite a sight themselves. Cal wore a black waistcoat and a tall silk top hat. Maggie looked positively regal in a midnight blue brocade gown. "You all look beautiful," Maggie said, smiling at her guests.

"So do you," Bess said. Her voice was dreamy. "I feel like a horse-drawn carriage will come at any moment to carry us off to the ball."

Cal cleared his throat, trying not to laugh. "I'm afraid we're fresh out of horses," he said apologetically. "And since cars are banned from town tonight, I suggest we start walking. That is, if George is ready to."

"Try and stop me," George said. Then she opened the front door, lifted her skirt, and skipped down the porch steps.

Cal held his arm out to his wife. "Shall we?" Bess and Nancy followed the Larsens as they walked in a stately manner out of the house.

Cal and Maggie lived about half a mile from the

center of town. The walk through the twilit streets was enchanting. One by one, the gas lamps were lit as darkness fell. Occasionally, the door to one of the houses would open, and a family would step out, dressed in elegant turn-of-the-century clothing. Nancy felt as if they had indeed stepped into another era in time. She caught her breath as they entered the center of town.

"It's like stepping into the middle of a play!" George exclaimed softly.

Everywhere they looked, there were women in full, flowing skirts and men in top hats and long, formal coats. Light, lilting music floated through the air.

"That's coming from the orchestra in the park," Maggie said. "There's dancing all night long. Why don't you girls start there? Cal and I will catch up with you later."

Nancy, George, and Bess made their way through the park, greeting others dressed for the evening.

"Everyone's so polite," George noted. "It's almost as if we're all on good behavior or something since we're wearing these clothes."

"It's true," Bess said with a giggle. "All these men are bowing like crazy and saying things like, 'Good evening, fair lady.' What a riot!"

Nancy laughed, wondering what her boyfriend,

Ned Nickerson, would look like all dressed up. Ned was naturally polite, but she couldn't quite imagine him acting so formal.

A small orchestra played on the bandstand, and all around them couples were whirling under the moonlight.

"I was hoping I'd see you here," said a lovely young woman in a light green dress edged with silver beadwork.

"Dana!" Nancy exclaimed. "I almost didn't recognize you with your hair all done up."

"I'm glad it was worthwhile," Dana said with a wry smile. "It took me two hours to do. Jesse, of course, was no help."

"Is he here tonight?" Nancy asked.

"Are you kidding? I don't think Jesse's come into town since he moved up to the refuge."

"Good evening, ladies." A tall, blond man doffed his top hat and gave them a low, graceful bow. Nancy just stared. She'd always thought Lucas Vaughn was handsome, but tonight he looked like the hero of a romantic novel.

"I don't think I've ever seen you look so beautiful, Miss Walsh," he said. He was clearly enjoying the role of a Victorian gentleman. "Will you do me the honor of a dance?"

"I shouldn't," Dana said, laughing, "but they say

Gaslight Night is charmed. I suppose I'll risk it."
She held out one gloved hand, and Lucas swept her
into the dance.

"Do you think it's true?" Bess asked. "That
tonight is charmed?"

"No," George said a moment later as Dana angrily broke away from Lucas. "Or if it was, the charm
just snapped. Do you think he threatened her
again?"

"I'm going to find out," Nancy said, heading
toward the dancers.

But before she could reach Dana, Cal Larsen
appeared at her side. "May I?" he asked, taking her
arm and whirling her into the group of dancers
before she could answer. Nancy was about to explain that she wanted to ask Dana a question when
Maggie broke in.

"Excuse me, Nancy," she said, "but there's
something I thought Cal would want to hear."

"What is it, Maggie?" Cal asked, frowning.

"I ran into Harry from the *Sentinel*. Word's just
come in. Those two escaped convicts who were still
free split up, and one was caught. But there's still
one man on the loose. He's stolen a gun, and the
police think he's not far from Seven Rocks."

9

Abducted!

One dance came to an end and another began as Nancy listened to Maggie's news. She hadn't really paid much attention to the story of the escaped convicts before. Now a sixth sense told her that somehow they were linked to her own case.

"I'm sorry, Maggie," Cal said, "but I'm afraid I'd better go over to the *Sentinel*."

"The story of my life," Maggie said with a resigned sigh. She kissed her husband and smiled. "Try to make it back before the last dance."

"Cal," Nancy said quickly, "would it be all right if I came with you?"

Cal gestured at the dancers whirling around the orchestra. "The night's still young, Nancy. You

89

haven't even been to one of the performances yet. Why would you want to leave this for a stuffy newspaper office?"

"I don't know," Nancy said honestly. "It's just a feeling I have that somehow this may be linked to my case. Call it a hunch."

Cal's brown eyes twinkled. "Dressed for a Victorian ball and still the diligent detective. You're Carson Drew's daughter, all right. Very well, come along if you like."

Nancy almost regretted her decision as she and Cal walked through the streets of Seven Rocks to the newspaper offices. Under the soft yellow glow of gaslights, the town's old wooden buildings seemed as if they'd never known the modern world. Nancy gasped as a dashingly dressed couple rode by on two bay horses. The woman, who wore a riding habit with a black top hat, was actually riding sidesaddle.

The *Sentinel's* offices were housed in a solid brick two-story building on the north end of town. Nancy followed Cal into the large, brightly lit newsroom. Several people were working at computers. Others scanned long sheets of newsprint. Most of them nodded to Cal. A few made jokes about his wardrobe taking a definite turn for the better.

Cal spoke briefly with a young man wearing

wire-rimmed glasses, who gave him a yellow sheet of paper. Cal studied the paper for a moment and then handed it to Nancy. "Have a look at this," he said, removing his top hat and coat. "It's a copy of the police bulletin on the two convicts."

Nancy read quickly. The bulletin contained basic information on each of the two men, along with photographs of each. A tall, dark-haired man named Roy Haines had been apprehended about fifty miles from Seven Rocks. Still on the loose was a fair-haired man with fine features that were almost familiar to Nancy. She gasped when she read his name: Alex "The Cat" Catlin.

Nancy quickly took in the rest of the bulletin. Catlin had a string of convictions. Before his escape he'd been doing time for armed robbery. The police were fairly sure that he'd recently stolen a gun from a town approximately twenty miles from Seven Rocks. The report ended with the words, "Catlin is considered armed and dangerous."

"All right," Cal said briskly. "We'll use this as the lead story for tomorrow's edition. Harry, do you have anything else on this?"

The young man pushed back a shock of thick brown hair. "Sorry, Cal," answered the young man. "That's all that came in."

Cal frowned. "If this guy is really near Seven

Rocks, I wonder if the police shouldn't make some sort of announcement. After all, the entire town is out there right now celebrating Gaslight Night. That means we've got a town full of empty houses. There couldn't be a sweeter setup for a convict."

Harry stood up, looking alarmed. "You're right. I'll spread the word right now."

"Sit down." Cal said abruptly. "If this guy *isn't* near Seven Rocks, and someone makes an announcement like that, then we're needlessly ruining everyone's evening. The last thing I want is a town of panicked people. Catlin might not even be close."

Nancy had only been half-listening to their conversation. She couldn't get past Catlin's nickname. At last she said, "I don't think we have to worry about whether or not the Cat is going to show up in Seven Rocks. He's been here for the last week."

Cal looked stunned for a moment. Then he dropped into a chair. "Of course," he said quietly. "The sign of the cat. Catlin's the one who's been sabotaging the refuge." His face paled as he added, "Good heavens. That means he's also the one who left the bear trap for us. Nancy, he's after *you*."

Nancy's heart was already pounding, but she took several deep breaths, forcing herself to remain calm. "I think that was just a warning," she said.

"After all, no one was hurt. And, as far as we know, the Cat hasn't struck anywhere since then."

"Maybe he's left Seven Rocks altogether," Harry suggested.

"Not likely," Cal said. "There's something he wants that's connected to Paws."

"Cal," Nancy said, "do you have any reports of a stolen blue pickup with a gun rack? Sergeant Baker said she'd check, but I haven't heard from her yet."

Cal gave Harry a nod, and Harry typed in a few commands on his keyboard. Seconds later, a list appeared on his computer screen. "Nothing in Seven Rocks," he reported. "Or Byerstown. Or Clark."

"The two closest towns," Cal interrupted for Nancy. "Go a little farther out, Harry."

Harry pressed another key, then gave a low whistle. "Two days after the breakout at the prison, a vehicle that fits that description was reported missing in Shadow Creek. That's about fourteen miles from Griffin, where the federal prison is."

"That doesn't help us," Nancy said, unable to hide her disappointment. "Catlin was already *here* by then. The bear was released the day after the breakout."

"You're overlooking one critical thing," Cal pointed out. "The truck was *reported* missing two days after the breakout. That doesn't mean it wasn't stolen earlier. The owner could have been away for two days and not discovered the theft until he returned home."

Nancy nodded at the computer screen. "Will that tell us?"

"Sorry," Harry said. "For minor crimes so far away, all we get is a list—no details. But I can call in to Griffin's paper, the *Gazette*, and see if they can help us out."

Harry made the call and hung up a few minutes later. "No luck. They've only got a skeleton staff on at this hour. They told me to check back in the morning."

"Okay," Nancy said, mentally reviewing the facts so far. "There's a good chance that Catlin stole the blue pickup. Which means that he's probably the one who tried to run George and me off the road. He must have been up at the refuge two days ago, too."

"That comforts me to no end," Cal said in a dry tone. He gave Nancy a stern, fatherly look. "Catlin clearly wants you off the case. I'm afraid I'm going to have to insist. We can't have anything harmful happen to you. Catlin is an extremely dangerous man."

"I've never been scared off a case before," Nancy

said quietly. "And I'm not going to be scared off now."

"Nancy—"

"Please, Cal," she broke in. "Why don't we call Sergeant Baker and tell her what we know?"

Cal reached for a phone. "All right," he muttered as he punched in the number for the police station.

Cal asked for Sergeant Baker and hung up a few minutes later. "Sergeant Baker and the rest of the police department are out patrolling the celebration."

Nancy sat down on top of an empty desk. "The entire police department?" she asked.

"We only have five police officers," Harry said. "Seven Rocks is a small town."

"Who answered the phone?" Nancy asked.

Cal rubbed his forehead. "Night deskman. He said he'd try to get a message to Sergeant Baker as fast as he could. But I'd feel better if I talked to Sergeant Baker in person," Cal said.

Nancy could feel a familiar eagerness. The pieces of the puzzle were beginning to fall into place. She didn't know what would happen next, but she knew that she had to be part of the action. "You've got a front page to prepare for tomorrow," she told Cal and Harry. "Why don't you let me find Sergeant Baker? I'll bring her back here with me."

Cal glowered at her from beneath thick white brows. "I thought we'd just established the fact that Alex Catlin is after you."

"He probably won't appear in town tonight," Nancy said. "The streets are filled with people."

"All right," Cal said reluctantly. "Go find Sergeant Baker. But take Harry with you. And please —be careful."

Nancy was glad Cal had suggested that Harry accompany her. The young reporter knew the town well and kept her amused with stories about Seven Rocks' more colorful characters.

Though Harry was not in costume, Nancy found herself caught up once again in the festive spell of the evening. On the school lawn, the seventh grade was performing a skit about Isabella Bird, the British woman who rode through the Rockies in the 1870s. A mule race was being held on the football field by a group of men dressed as prospectors. And in front of the Silver Dollar Saloon, a man with a banjo was singing a ballad.

Harry looked around at the townspeople strolling the streets. "Sergeant Baker could be anywhere." Nancy and Harry were almost at the southern edge of the town. "Two more blocks, and we're in the residential section," Harry said. "I don't see that many people down here. Why don't we turn around and try another street?"

Nancy considered his advice. "It won't take long just to go to the end of the street," she said. "Especially since it's not so crowded here."

Harry agreed, and they continued down Market Street. The street was darker here. They passed a sporting goods store and a fabric store.

"Maybe we should keep an eye out for someone who looks like Catlin," Harry said.

"If he's here, he'd be easy to spot. He'd be one of the only ones out of costume," Nancy said.

Suddenly, Harry let out a low moan.

Nancy turned to see the young reporter sink to his knees.

"Harry, what is it?" she cried.

Harry never answered. Instead, a thick cloth with a sickening smell was clamped over Nancy's nose and mouth. Struggling, she fought for air. Then she felt a brief spinning sensation, and the world went black.

10

On the Mountain

The moon was still up, but the sky was turning light gray when Nancy woke. She opened her eyes to see a canopy of evergreens above her. Somewhere not too far away, coyotes were howling. She could smell damp earth and pine trees—and the lingering odor of whatever it was that had been used to knock her out.

I'm somewhere in the mountains, Nancy thought woozily. She was shivering and achy. Even though she was lying down, she felt dizzy. She tried to sit up and realized at once that she couldn't. Her hands were tied behind her back, and thick ropes bound her ankles.

I am not going to panic, Nancy told herself firmly. I am going to get out of this.

Nancy lay still, listening for any sign of whoever had brought her there. After what seemed like hours, she was finally convinced that she was alone. Now she could begin the slow process of trying to sit up.

She tried raising her upper body, but even all the sit-ups she'd done with George were no help with her hands bound behind her. All she could do was raise her head and shoulders off the ground. And that completely exhausted her.

Nancy lay on her side for a few moments, getting her breath back. For the first time, she realized she was still wearing the dress she'd rented from Nellie's. The lovely ivory silk was covered with mud and pine needles.

It's going to be a lot of fun trying to explain this to Nellie, Nancy thought. "I'm sorry, but while I was wearing your gown, I was abducted, tied up with ropes, and woke up covered with mud on a mountainside."

Maybe sitting up would be easier if she used a tree for support. She inched over to the nearest pine by bending her knees and pushing off with her heels, all the while trying to ignore the pain of the ropes cutting into her wrists and ankles.

Nancy pressed her shoulders against the rough bark. Inch by inch, she began to push herself up. The bark scraped her already aching wrists. Forget the pain, she told herself. You've been through worse.

At last she was sitting up. Her heart raced from the effort. For a few minutes, Nancy remained perfectly still, waiting for her breathing to return to normal. The question now was how to get rid of the ropes.

Directly ahead of her, about fifty feet uphill, was an outcrop of bedrock. From where she was sitting, the edges on the rock looked sharp. They might not be sharp enough to slice through the ropes, Nancy realized, but they were the only chance she had.

By stretching her legs out, digging her heels into the soft earth, and pushing herself upward, Nancy made slow progress up the hill. Twice she fell over and had to repeat the process of righting herself against a tree. Her arms and legs ached from the tight ropes.

Finally, Nancy reached the rocks, her energy spent. She dropped her head against her knees and rested, trying to catch her breath.

The soft call of a bird made her raise her head. Perched on the rock above her was a small brown bird. It looked at her curiously with bright black eyes.

"You're not used to seeing people in this condition, are you?" Nancy asked.

The bird cocked its head, as if considering her question.

"Well, I'm not used to this, either," Nancy said. Somehow, hearing her own voice in the still forest made her feel better. "So," she said to the bird, "what do you think I should do?"

In answer, the bird spread its wings and took flight, soaring high into the sky.

Nancy laughed, her courage restored. "A very good idea," she said. Then she turned her back to the sharp edge of the rock and began the slow process of sawing through the ropes that bound her hands.

Nancy didn't know how long it took her to cut through the ropes. But by the time she freed herself, the sky had lightened and a cold drizzle was falling. She rubbed her arms and legs, wincing at the pain as her circulation was restored. Finally, she stood up, holding on to the rocks for support.

"A little dizzy," she observed, "but otherwise okay." The first thing to do was to get her bearings. She was on a mountain somewhere in the Rockies. And since she was pretty sure it was the morning after Gaslight Night, whoever had brought her here couldn't have taken her that far from Seven Rocks. She looked around, trying to get a sense of direction. The sun rose in the east, she knew, but that did her no good because she had no idea which direction she wanted to go. At last she decided to try to find a trail or drinking water or both. And it would be easier to start by walking downhill.

The drizzle became rain as Nancy made her way down the mountain. Muddy water squished through her shoes. My dress pumps, Nancy thought in dismay.

She was lost, cold, hungry, and tired. It didn't help to be walking in heels and what felt like at least twenty pounds of soaking wet silk and petticoats. Nancy shivered and rubbed her arms to warm them. Think about something other than the cold, she told herself.

As Nancy inched her way carefully over the slippery rocks and mud of the mountainside, she wondered who had abducted her and why. Alex Catlin was the obvious answer, but would someone that dangerous have left her alive? Had he followed her during all of Gaslight Night? Had he been following her for days? Again she wondered why he'd been sabotaging Paws. Was it Dana he was after? Or Jesse? And what had happened to poor Harry? Whoever abducted her must have hit Harry on the head. Nancy hoped he was safe. Cal and Maggie were probably frantic by now, she thought with regret.

There was a sudden snap as the heel on one of Nancy's shoes broke. Then her foot slid out from under her, and she was tumbling head over heels down the mountain.

Nancy came to a thumping stop, lying facedown on the wet earth. She rolled over onto her side and winced at the pain in her knee, where she had hit it on a sharp rock. "Things can't get much worse than this," Nancy said to herself.

A low growl told her she had spoken too soon.

Slowly, Nancy lifted her head to stare into the eyes of a very large cinnamon-colored bear. She shut her eyes briefly, hoping she'd imagined it. When she opened them again the bear was still there, no more than seventy-five feet away.

Slowly, the bear began to move toward her. Nancy felt her muscles constrict with terror. Frantically, she tried to recall the advice in Maggie's guidebook. What was it you were supposed to do when confronted by a bear? Keep eye contact or look down? Talk softly or make a lot of noise? Remain perfectly still or run?

She couldn't remember. She couldn't move. Suddenly, Nancy realized that she might never make it off the mountain.

Nancy stared at the bear, frozen with fear. The huge animal made a low rumbling sound in its throat. It was moving more quickly now, closing the distance between them. It would reach her at any moment.

Somehow, Nancy's muscles relaxed, and her voice returned. "Easy," she said in as calm a voice as she could manage. "Just stay where you are. I'll get out of your way."

The bear took no notice of her words. It loped toward her, straight and determined.

Moving as smoothly as possible so as not to startle the animal, Nancy rose to her knees. Then, very slowly, she got to her feet. If she remained lying on the ground, she'd have no chance. From the bear's point of view, she'd be easy prey. If she was lucky, she'd be able to get to a tree. Of course, climbing it in the sodden gown would be another story.

The bear stopped as Nancy drew herself to her full height. Then, as if mimicking her, the animal rose on its hind legs. There were now only a few yards between them. The bear opened its mouth to growl, revealing sharp, yellowed teeth. Nancy's heart was racing, and her knees shook.

A loud thunking sound ripped through the woods, and Nancy screamed, startled by the noise.

The bear stood still, as if stunned. Then Nancy saw that it had been shot with a tranquilizer. She held her breath, wondering how quickly the drug would take effect. The bear seemed to be distracted by the shot, and Nancy took this opportunity to take a slow, silent step backward. The bear noticed her movement and let out a low growl.

Nancy knew the bear wouldn't be able to stand on its hind legs for long, and she feared that when it landed on its front legs, she would be pinned underneath it. When the bear took a faltering step forward, Nancy bolted to her right, behind a thick tree. A second later, the bear swayed—and fell.

Nancy gazed at the fallen animal in disbelief. It was breathing, but it didn't have the strength to run. Still shaken, she looked past the bear.

Jesse McKay leaned against a fir tree, holding a tranquilizer gun in one hand. He was wearing a green slicker and a backpack, and he was looking at her with contempt.

"What are you doing here?" he asked in his usual hostile tone.

"Enjoying the great outdoors," Nancy snapped back.

Jesse actually grinned. "Great hiking clothes," he observed.

Nancy smiled in spite of herself. At the moment, she was almost happy to see Jesse McKay. After all, he *had* rescued her from a bear. "What are *you* doing here?" she asked.

"Looking for him," the boy answered, jerking his head toward the bear. The animal could make only feeble movements, now that the drug was taking full effect. He pointed to an angry-looking gash on the bear's hip, and Nancy saw the remains of a gauze bandage.

"This is the bear that was let out of the refuge?" Nancy asked in surprise.

Jesse nodded.

"But it's not black!"

"Not all black bears are black," Jesse said patiently. "Most are brown. But they can vary in color from cinnamon, like this one, to true black. Some even have white patches."

"Oh," Nancy said. Some part of her mind noticed that the rain had stopped after Jesse appeared.

"Are you all right?" he asked. He walked toward Nancy, really looking at her for the first time. "What happened to you, anyway?"

"I was abducted," Nancy said, amazed by the change in his attitude.

Jesse's gray eyes took in the scrapes along her arms. He nodded at a nearby log. "Why don't you sit down? I've got some water and munchies in my pack. And I'll see what I can do about those cuts."

Nancy did as he suggested, settling herself in a rustle of wet silk. Jesse handed her a water bottle and a bag of trail mix. Then he took antiseptic from the pack. Carefully, he cleaned and bandaged her scrapes. "Now," he said, "I'm going to have a look at that bear. And you're going to tell me what happened."

Jesse worked on the unconscious bear as Nancy told her story. The boy seemed totally absorbed by the bear. As she talked he removed the old bandage and cleaned and dressed the gash. Finally, he reached inside the pack, took out a hypodermic needle, and gave the animal an injection.

"Antibiotic," he explained. "He got himself infected all over again."

"Did you hear anything I just said?" Nancy asked, annoyed.

"Yeah," he said, getting to his feet. "You were abducted in that ridiculous dress, but you're basically fine."

"Jesse," Nancy said patiently, "an escaped convict named Alex Catlin is the one who's been sabotaging Paws. Doesn't that mean anything to you?"

Jesse gave her a reckless grin. "Yeah, we probably ought to adopt a few Dobermans."

"What about the note and the envelope?" Nancy asked, refusing to be put off.

Jesse shrugged. "What about it?"

"I don't think Alex Catlin is after Dana," Nancy said. "I think he's after you."

For a split second Jesse's gray eyes darkened with

something like fury. Then, just as quickly, the expression was gone. "If he wants to leave notes, that's his problem," he said in a casual tone.

It was all Nancy could do not to lose her temper. "Jesse," she said, "you're not the only one in danger. If you won't think about Dana or me, at least think about the animals. Alex Catlin is threatening everything you love."

Jesse didn't answer, but his eyes looked cold and hard.

"Please," Nancy urged. "I'm trying to help you. You have to tell me why Alex Catlin is after you."

"Have to?" Jesse repeated. He shook his head. "No, Ms. Detective. The only thing *I* have to do is get this bear back to the refuge before he regains consciousness." His voice was steely. "And if you know what's good for you, you'll keep your nose out of my business."

11

An Unexpected Clue

Nancy stood up angrily and faced Jesse. "Are you threatening me?"

The boy gave a bored shrug. "No."

She looked at him in amazement. "Honestly, the bear was easier to talk to than you are!"

"Yeah, I saw you talking to the bear," Jesse said. "That was real impressive." He knelt and drew an ax from his pack. "Don't you know the only way to scare off a bear is to make a lot of noise? You're supposed to bang on pots and pans or something."

"Silly me," Nancy said. "I left all my pots and pans home."

Jesse gave her another grin, went over to a thin sapling, and began chopping at its base.

"What are you doing?" Nancy asked. She realized that talking to Jesse about Alex Catlin was useless.

"Making a travois to carry the bear," Jesse replied.

Nancy gathered up the skirt of her dress and did her best to wring it out. "How do you plan on getting the bear back to Paws?"

"I need help," Jesse said. "That's a full-grown male black bear. It probably weighs between three and four hundred pounds. You didn't think you and I were going to carry this bear by ourselves, did you?"

"Who will know that you've found him?" Nancy asked, ignoring his question.

"Dana's worked out a system," Jesse replied. "If someone from Paws finds an animal like this, he alerts her, and she calls the volunteer team. Then there's about five of us to move the animal."

"So you want me to go back to Paws and get help?" Nancy asked.

"I don't know," Jesse said thoughtfully. He nodded toward the sleeping bear. "I'd rather not leave him here unprotected. He's going to wake up in a while. But you had a rough night. And we're almost two miles from the refuge. There's a trail, but it's uphill all the way and pretty steep. It could take a couple of hours. Are you up for that?"

"I think so," Nancy told him. At least she'd have a chance to warn Dana about what was going on.

Jesse frowned at her dress. "I don't have a change of clothes. Do you want to take my rain slicker?"

"No thanks," Nancy said. "I can't bear the idea of putting on another piece of clothing." She looked down at her broken shoe. "How about your sneakers?" she joked.

"Forget it. Your feet are too small." But Jesse gave her one of his rare smiles and carefully showed her how to find the trail.

As Jesse had warned, the trail that led to the refuge was steep. In fact, it rose nearly straight up the mountainside. There were places where Nancy had to hold on to roots or branches to pull herself up. She soon decided it was easier to walk barefoot than to walk with one shoe that didn't have a heel. She picked her way along the trail, watching out for sharp stones and sticks.

This isn't exactly what I had in mind when I planned to go hiking in the Rockies, Nancy thought. She dropped to the ground beneath an aspen tree to take a short break. Above her the golden leaves brushed against each other in the wind. A few swirled to the ground. Nancy took a deep drink of the water Jesse had given her.

Jesse McKay. There was a true puzzle. A boy

whose moods changed faster than lightning. Hostile and angry one minute, gentle and concerned the next. Sergeant Baker's words came back to her once more: "He's hiding something." And whatever that is, Nancy thought, it's connected to Alex Catlin.

Feeling more rested, she stood up and continued on her way. The sun was already high in the sky. It must be close to noon, Nancy figured. Where was Alex Catlin now? she wondered, hoping he wasn't hiding in the mountains nearby. She was willing to bet that he hadn't left Seven Rocks. And somehow, she was equally sure that he still hadn't been captured.

At length the trail forked. Nancy took the right fork, as Jesse had instructed. A short while later, she veered right again onto the narrow footpath that led to the refuge.

Dana caught sight of her just as Nancy emerged from the woods. Dana's jaw dropped in surprise, and the heavy bag of feed she was carrying slid from her hands. "What happened to you?" she cried, rushing to Nancy's side. "Are you all right? Bess and George and the Larsens are worried sick! And why are you barefoot?"

"I'm fine," Nancy said, laughing with relief. She told Dana the whole story.

Dana put a comforting arm around her shoulder. "Come inside with me. First we'll call Cal and

Maggie and tell everyone you're all right. Then I'll call the rescue team. And then we'll get you out of that dress."

Dana led Nancy into the library of the mansion. "Here," she said, holding out the phone. "Convince them you're still alive."

Nancy talked with Bess and George and both Maggie and Cal. The cousins insisted on driving up to Paws at once to bring Nancy back.

"Whew!" Nancy said when the conversation was over. "I never meant for everyone to get that scared."

"Weren't *you*?" Dana asked in disbelief.

"Only when I found your bear." Nancy looked around at the bookshelves crammed with old leather-bound volumes. Now that she was feeling better, her natural curiosity had returned. "Dana," she said, "what are all these old books?"

Dana waved a careless hand at the shelves. "Mostly books on wildlife and botany that my great-grandmother collected." She picked one out at random and handed it to Nancy. "See for yourself. I'm going to make those calls."

Carefully, Nancy examined the yellowed pages. The book was highly technical, written for scientists. Nancy returned the book to its place, her eyes browsing the other titles. As Dana had said, almost all the books were about wildlife or plants.

113

"I'm going to get you something else to wear," Dana announced, her calls finished. "There's food in the kitchen, if you want. Help yourself."

But Nancy wasn't interested in food. A tall, thin book on one of the lower shelves caught her interest. *A Pictorial History of Seven Rocks,* the title read. The copyright date was 1910, and the book was filled with sepia-tinted photographs of the town in its early years.

"Try these on," Dana said, returning to the library with a pair of blue sweatpants and a white sweatshirt. "I'm afraid they're all I have that's clean. With all the excitement, I haven't had a chance to do laundry."

"They're perfect," Nancy said. "Thanks."

Dana glanced at the book Nancy had picked out. "The text is a little boring, but those old photos are fun."

"Would it be all right if I borrowed it?" Nancy asked. "I'll bring it back in a day or so."

"Help yourself," Dana said as the doorbell rang. "That must be Bess and George."

Nancy had just finished changing when Bess and George rushed into the library.

"Oh, Nancy!" Bess cried, hugging her friend. "We're so glad you're safe!" Her eyes went to the crumpled heap of silk and lace on the floor. "Oh . . . the dress."

Nancy winced. "I know. What am I going to tell Nellie?"

"Don't worry," Bess said brightly. "I returned the other dresses this morning, and I talked to Nellie. She showed me all these magazines from the turn of the century. The fashions were incredible. Anyway," Bess went on, "Nellie is really nice. I'm sure she'll understand."

Nancy wasn't entirely convinced, but she decided to leave the matter up to Bess. There were other things on her mind. "Do either of you know what happened to Harry, the *Sentinel* reporter?"

"He's got a nasty concussion, but Dr. Yan says he's going to be fine," George said. "Sergeant Baker and Cal found him near the end of Market Street."

"That's where we were attacked," Nancy said. "Did Harry remember anything about how it happened?"

George shook her head. "He was hit from behind. The police found a cloth reeking of ether nearby."

"That's what knocked me out," Nancy said. She shivered, remembering the moment when the cloth had come down over her mouth and nose.

"Let's get you home," George said.

Nancy picked up the book, then turned to Dana. "When you and Lucas were dancing last night, what did he say that made you break away?"

Dana leaned against the desk, twisting the end of her long braid. "Oh, nothing new. He told me again he wanted me to tone down my campaign."

"But he didn't threaten you?" Nancy asked.

"No," Dana said. "He was just being his usual irritating self."

"Alex Catlin is our problem," Nancy said with certainty. "Dana, we've got to find him before he does more damage. Until we do, it's not safe for you to stay up here. Why don't you come back to town with us?"

"I'm not leaving the animals," Dana said firmly. "They're in danger, too."

"Dana," Nancy pressed, "Alex Catlin is after Jesse. Don't you remember that first note? He said he was going to take him apart. He's going to keep coming back here until he does."

Dana turned to the leaded-glass window and stared out into the forest. "That's a risk I'll have to take."

Nancy sank back in the car seat and leafed through the pages of the old book Dana had lent her. "These pictures are amazing," she said to George and Bess. "In 1864, Market Street had only three buildings: a general store, a post office, and a millinery. And here's one of Evangeline Walsh. Maybe she's related to Dana. She's got this huge,

116

old camera. It looks like she's trying to take a picture of a fox." Nancy lifted her head from the book and realized they'd entered the town. "George," she said, "I don't think we ought to go straight to the Larsens'."

"You need to rest," Bess said from the backseat.

"I also need to talk to Sergeant Baker," Nancy explained. "I want to see if there's been any more news on Alex Catlin."

George turned toward the police station. Nancy's attention was drawn back to the book. "Here's a picture of Phineas in front of the Midnight Mine," she said. "He looks so proud."

As George pulled up in front of the police station, Nancy noticed something in the picture she hadn't seen before. The entrance to the mine was the same wooden structure that was now boarded up. But in Phineas's day, there was also an opening on the side. At least it looked that way. It was hard to tell from the old photograph.

"Oh," Nancy breathed. "I think I know how our 'ghost' disappeared!"

12

Jesse's Secret

"What ghost?" Bess asked, leaning over the back-seat to look at the photograph. "Do you mean Phineas?"

"I mean whoever it was I saw that day we were up at the mine," Nancy answered. "Somehow, I doubt it's Phineas. Look." She passed the book over to Bess. "I think that might be another entrance on the side there. Maybe that's how he got inside."

Bess squinted at the photograph. "I don't know," she said doubtfully. "This picture isn't all that clear."

"Still," Nancy said, "we probably should check it out."

"Now?" George asked. She had just parked in front of the police station.

"I guess it can wait," Nancy admitted, feeling a little disappointed. "I really should talk to Sergeant Baker."

Sergeant Baker looked up from her desk as the three girls entered the station. "Cal called and told me you were safe," she said. She looked pleased to see them. "I don't mind telling you, you had this department turned inside out. You're Seven Rocks' first abduction in twenty years."

"What a record," Bess said with a giggle.

"It is," Sergeant Baker agreed in a serious tone. "We're very lucky to have so little crime here. We have the odd theft or fight, but we haven't had to deal with anything like having Alex Catlin on the loose."

"Do you have any idea of where he might be hiding?" Nancy asked.

"It's a good bet he's not in town. As you've probably noticed, everyone in Seven Rocks knows everyone else. Most people even know the tourists. I don't think Catlin could hide out here." She pointed to a map on the wall that showed Seven Rocks and the surrounding Rocky Mountain wilderness. "However, he could be anywhere in the mountains."

"That doesn't exactly narrow it down," George said with a sigh.

"No," Sergeant Baker agreed. "Tell me what

happened to you, Nancy. Maybe there's a clue in your story."

Once again, Nancy related what happened after she left the newspaper's offices. Sergeant Baker took a few notes but did not interrupt. At last the police officer said, "I wouldn't have expected Jesse McKay to be so helpful."

"Neither did I," Nancy admitted. "I think you're right, though. He's definitely hiding something. You should have seen his reaction when I mentioned Alex Catlin."

Sergeant Baker tapped a pencil against her desk. "I'll question him when he gets back to Paws. Will you call me if you think of anything else?"

Nancy said she would. As the girls started to leave the station, Nancy turned back with one last question. "Sergeant Baker," she began, "a few nights ago someone saw the ghost of Phineas Armbruster at the Midnight Mine."

"Oh, that old legend," the police officer said with a laugh. "Every western town has a ghost story. That's ours, I'm afraid."

"Have there been any sightings since then?" Nancy asked.

Sergeant Baker looked puzzled, but when she saw that Nancy was serious, she simply said, "No. Not that I'm aware of."

Nancy sighed. "All right, then. Thanks, anyway."

After returning to the Larsens', Nancy took a shower and fell into a delicious nap. She awoke to hear Maggie Larsen knocking on the bedroom door.

"Nancy!" Maggie called. "Are you awake? Dana's on the phone for you. She says it's important."

The clock on the bedside table read a quarter after three. Nancy got up and put on a light robe. Then she hurried into the hallway to take the phone.

"He struck again," Dana said without any introduction.

"The Cat?" Nancy asked.

"He didn't leave his symbol this time." Dana's voice held no emotion.

"Are you all right?" Nancy asked.

"Poison," she answered. Dana spoke so softly, Nancy wasn't sure she'd heard it correctly. She could feel her own heart pounding. Dana sounded as if she were at wit's end.

"Please, Dana," she said, "tell me what happened."

Dana let out a ragged sob. "This afternoon, after Jesse and the others got back with the bear, I went out to the large-animal compound to give it some medication. And I saw the mountain lion tearing at a piece of meat—"

"That you didn't feed her," Nancy finished.

"We feed the animals early in the morning," Dana said. "I tried to get the meat away from her, but trying to take food away from a hungry mountain lion . . ." Dana's voice trailed off. "She's unconscious now. Jesse's going to be brokenhearted if we can't save her."

"Where was he when this happened?" Nancy asked.

"I—I don't know," Dana stammered. "That's the other thing. After they brought in the bear, Jesse said he was going to the cottage to clean up. I went to find him after I saw the cat with the meat, and . . . Nancy, I think he's gone."

"Are you sure?"

"It's hard to tell with Jesse. He doesn't have many things. The cottage always seems empty to me. But his pack was gone. Oh, Nancy, what if I've been wrong about him all along? What if Jesse *was* behind the sabotage here at Paws?"

"You can't believe that," Nancy said. "Jesse would sooner take his own life than hurt that cat. You know the way he feels about animals."

"I guess you're right," Dana said in a hollow voice. "I just don't know what to think anymore. But this refuge has become a dangerous place for the animals we're supposedly sheltering."

"Listen to me, Dana," Nancy said quickly. "Alex

Catlin has struck again. You've got to call Sergeant Baker and tell her what's happened. And then you've got to get off that mountain. There's a good chance Catlin is still on the grounds."

"I'm not leaving," Dana said firmly.

Nancy ran a hand through her hair, wondering what to do next. "Will you do me a favor, Dana?" she asked. "Will you check the cottage again? This time, take note of *everything* you see. Maybe there'll be a clue to where Jesse's gone. And then call me back."

Dana agreed and hung up.

Nancy took a deep breath and leaned back against the wall. She'd known that the Cat would strike again, but she'd never guessed it would happen this fast. Nancy hadn't let Dana know her worst fear. Maybe Jesse hadn't left. Maybe Jesse was taken against his will.

Nancy walked back to the bedroom and stood in front of the mirror, barely noticing her own reflection. Quickly, she brushed her hair back and pulled it into a neat ponytail. She changed into jeans, sneakers, and a light yellow pullover sweater. Dana hadn't called back yet, but that hadn't changed Nancy's plan. She hoped that Bess and George were somewhere in the house. If they went to Paws with her, it would probably be easier to persuade Dana to leave.

The bedroom door swung open, and George walked in, trailed by Munro. George still had a slight limp.

"You're up," George said cheerfully. "We all thought you'd sleep for days."

"In the middle of a case?" Nancy joked. Then her tone became serious as she told George about Dana's call.

"That's not good news," George said. "But I think you'll find my research very interesting."

"What research?" Nancy asked.

"Well, while certain people were sleeping through the afternoon," George began, "I decided to pay a visit to the *Sentinel*'s morgue. You know, where they keep back issues of their own paper and a few other papers."

"What did you find?"

George sat down on one of the beds and proudly held out a manila folder.

Nancy sat beside her and opened the folder. Inside were photographs of a series of articles from the Griffin *Gazette*. Written two years earlier, they covered the trial of Alex Catlin.

Nancy emitted a low whistle as she skimmed the first article. "He's got a string of arrests and convictions going back to when he was ten years old. 'Breaking and entering, arson, assault, robbery . . .'" she read. "But even with all those convictions, it wasn't until this trial that he actually got jail time."

"Keep reading," George said. "You haven't gotten to the really interesting part."

"'The trial favored the defense,'" Nancy read, "'until the appearance of a surprise witness, Catlin's younger brother, Jesse, age sixteen. "Jesse Catlin's testimony turned the trial around," said a member of the jury later. "Jesse Catlin convicted his own brother."'"

Nancy glanced at the accompanying photographs. "That's his secret," Nancy said. "Jesse McKay is really Jesse Catlin!"

13

The Cat's Lair

Nancy stared at the photograph of Jesse, which had been taken two years earlier. He was wearing a stiff-looking suit and tie, but he was unmistakably Jesse. No wonder Alex had seemed so familiar. Although heavier, Alex had the same finely chiseled features.

The phone rang again. "I'll get it," George said. She reappeared almost immediately. "Nancy, it's Dana."

"I went back to the cottage," Dana said when Nancy had picked up the phone. "All I found were a couple of T-shirts, a bunch of rock tapes, some bug repellent, and a map."

"What does the map show?" Nancy asked.

126

"It's a topographic map of a section of the Rockies," Dana answered. "It's all mountain and forest. There are four spots that Jesse—or someone —circled in pencil."

"Alex Catlin and Jesse are brothers," Nancy told Dana. She paused, and there was silence on the other end of the phone.

"I don't believe it," Dana said finally.

"Jesse testified at Alex's trial and sent him to jail," Nancy went on. "I'm sure that's why Alex has been after him. What I don't know is whether Jesse left the refuge on his own—trying to outrun Alex —or whether Alex got him."

"You mean the way he got you?" Dana's voice quavered.

"Something like that," Nancy said. "Look, if Alex took him, I don't know what we can do. But if Jesse left under his own power, we should check out those four places on the map. Do you know where they are?"

"They all look like they're in deep woodland," Dana said. "And it's going to take time to check them out. They're miles apart from each other. We need to narrow them down to the most likely place Jesse went."

Nancy twirled the phone cord between her fingers. How could she narrow down four places on a map she couldn't even see? "I know," she said. "Maggie's an expert on that stuff. If you bring the map here, I'm sure she'll help us."

"Maggie's the best when it comes to trails," Dana agreed, "but I'm talking about wilderness. There isn't a single trail near any of these places." She gave a reluctant sigh. "I hate to do it, but I think we're going to have to ask Lucas for help. No one knows the mountains better. He'll be able to look at the map and tell us exactly what's at each spot."

"Do you think he will?" Nancy asked.

"He has to," Dana said simply. "Meet me at his place in forty-five minutes."

Nancy found George and Bess in the kitchen. Bess had just put a cake in the oven, and George was doing her best to clean the bowl. "Are you up for another visit to Vaughn Outfitters?" Nancy asked.

"Sure," George said.

Bess put down the wooden spoon. "I don't want to let you down, but I just put the cake in to bake."

"It's all right," Nancy said quickly. "Actually, it might be a good idea if you stayed here. We might need to call for backup."

Bess raised her hand in mock salute. "I'll be waiting," she said, "and so will a chocolate cake."

"That just leaves one problem. . . ." Nancy said. "Explaining this to Maggie and Cal." She knew that the Larsens had been worried by her ordeal. She wasn't sure how to tell them that now she had to search for Jesse.

"Maggie's at the post office," Bess said, "and Cal's at the *Sentinel*. Don't worry—I'll explain everything when they get home. Oh, I almost forgot. Cal stopped by while you were napping. He said to tell you there's been another sighting of Phineas at the Midnight. He said to ask if you wouldn't prefer to chase a nice, friendly ghost rather than an escaped convict."

Nancy's blue eyes sparkled with excitement. "Tell Cal I'm going to take him up on his idea."

"This isn't the way to Vaughn's," George said as Nancy steered the yellow rental car to the north end of Seven Rocks.

"Since we have a little time, I thought we'd take a detour," Nancy explained. "To the mine."

George looked at her friend in surprise. "You really do want to check out that ghost story."

"I keep thinking about the photograph in Dana's book," Nancy said. "It's hard to be sure, but it looked like there was a side entrance. And I know I saw a very real person go into the mine the first time we were there. I just couldn't figure out how he did it."

Nancy pulled up in front of the Midnight, parked the car, and took out her flashlight.

"You know," George said, getting out of the car and surveying the deserted area, "I think we're the only ones who ever visit this place. Old Phineas ought to be grateful for the company."

Nancy stood a short distance from the mine, the open book in her hand. "Let's see," she said, studying the photograph. "If this dark part sticking out here was an entrance, it would have been on the left side." She looked up at the low wooden building that led into the Midnight. Directly in front of her was the boarded-up door. Nancy consulted the book again, then walked around to the left side. There was no sign of another entrance. Thick wooden planks blackened with age formed a solid wall.

Carefully, Nancy examined them. She checked to see if any of the boards were loose or looked as if they could be moved.

"Any luck?" George said.

"No," Nancy replied. "I don't understand it. According to this, there was definitely something here besides blank wall."

"Maybe it was torn down and the wall was put up later," George suggested.

"That's possible," Nancy admitted. She stared once again at the sepia print. Her pulse quickened. "Or maybe the problem is the photograph."

"What do you mean?" George asked.

"Most photographs are printed from negatives," Nancy explained. "And it's easy to flip a negative— to print it the wrong way by mistake. If that's what happened in this book, then the second entrance was on the *right* side of the mine."

Immediately, Nancy and George circled to the right side of the wooden building. At first the wall looked identical to the other—old wooden planks, splintered and buckled by years of mountain weather. Then Nancy noticed what she hadn't seen before. Two of the planks were so severely buckled that they pushed out a few inches from the ground.

She knelt down and pulled on the first plank. It swung up and outward, about two feet from the ground. "George," Nancy said, "do you think a man could crawl through this opening?"

"I know I could." George glanced at her watch. "Do we have time? Aren't we supposed to meet Dana in about twenty minutes?"

"We'll just take a quick look," Nancy promised.

George stared at the raised board, puzzled. "Didn't you say you saw that man enter the mine— as in walk through an open door?"

"That's what it looked like." Nancy shrugged. "I don't understand it, either."

"You know, this place can't be too safe with all this rotten wood," George said.

Nancy looked at her friend and smiled. "Well, we

have at least two good reasons for *not* crawling inside—"

"And you want to do it, anyway," George finished for her, returning the smile.

Nancy nodded. "Don't you think it's interesting that Phineas's ghost has been turning up ever since the Cat came to Seven Rocks?"

George bit her lip. "You think Alex Catlin's inside? If he is, he must be sitting there waiting for us. We haven't exactly been quiet."

"No," Nancy said. "I think he'd let us know by now if he were here. I'm going inside."

George grinned and bowed, one hand sweeping toward the mine. "After you."

Holding her flashlight in front of her, Nancy crawled slowly into the dark space. The first thing she noticed was the years-old buildup of soot and dust. It went straight to the back of her throat. She wasn't more than a foot inside before she was coughing violently. Behind her the board swung shut, and she heard George coughing, too.

"We should have brought bandannas," George gasped.

"Too late now," Nancy said. She shone her flashlight around the small room that had once led into the silver mine. The air was damp and cool.

Suddenly, George jumped back, pointing ahead

of her. Her hand was pressed down over her mouth, stifling a scream.

Nancy looked in the direction George was pointing. A strange, furry mass was hanging from the ceiling. "They're just bats," Nancy told her. "They sleep holding on to each other. They won't hurt us."

"What if they fly into us?" George asked.

"They won't," Nancy assured her. "They're great at navigating. If we don't bump into them, they probably won't even wake up."

"If you say so," George said doubtfully.

The room became darker as the girls moved farther back. Then, in one wall, Nancy saw a sliver of light. "I think this is what we're looking for," she said. She pushed at the place where the light came through. The entire wooden board moved outward. "This is where he got in."

Once more, Nancy swung the flashlight. This time she saw the rest of the proof she needed. On the ground was a crumpled cigarette pack, an empty box of rifle shells, and a charcoal stick.

"He's definitely armed," Nancy said, shining the light on the box. "And that charcoal is what he drew the cat with," she said softly. "We've found the Cat's lair."

"Great. Let's get out of here before he returns," George said. "I don't like this place."

Nancy nodded toward the loosened board. "We might as well use his exit."

But as Nancy moved toward the opening, there was a loud crack. With lightning-fast reflexes, George pulled Nancy back. A ceiling beam thudded to the floor—landing exactly where Nancy had been standing a second earlier.

A thick cloud of dust filled the air, and both girls covered their faces, choking. As they turned toward the place where they had crawled in, a second beam fell.

Nancy couldn't see George in the blackness, but she heard her panicked voice. "Nancy, it's going to cave in!"

14

Alex Catlin

Nancy and George huddled on the floor of the Midnight Mine, coughing furiously. The air moved with a rush of wings above them.

"The bats!" George choked.

"Just stay low," Nancy rasped. She kept her head buried in her arms, breathing through her sleeve until the dust settled.

Several long minutes later, the girls could see and breathe again. The bats were gone, and two of the thick ceiling beams lay in front of them.

Nancy wiped the lens of her flashlight on her pants leg and shone it toward the ceiling. "We've got to get out of here before the rest of this place collapses." She looked toward where they'd crawled in. "Let's try to go back this way."

Moving cautiously, the two girls made their way through the abandoned building. At last they reached the loose board. Nancy's hands trembled as she pried it open. They couldn't risk any more of the Midnight falling apart. She held her breath as the board swung outward. Finally, she and George crawled out.

For a long moment, both girls lay on the ground, taking deep swallows of the fresh mountain air. Their eyes met at the same moment.

"Look at you!" George gasped. "Your hair and your face are completely black. And was that sweater really yellow?"

Nancy looked down at herself and groaned. "I don't seem to be having much luck with clothing lately. But you're no better."

George stood up and tried to brush off the layers of soot. "We should do a commercial for laundry detergent," she said.

"They haven't invented the detergent that would get rid of this dirt," Nancy replied. Her mind was already returning to the case. "George, I really do have to meet Dana. But someone should tell Sergeant Baker that we've found the Cat's hideout. Would you mind if I dropped you off at the station?"

"You want me to walk into a police station looking like this?"

Nancy shrugged. "I'm going to walk into Lucas's place. Please, George. It's important that the police know about this."

George sighed. "You know I will." She headed toward the yellow rental car. "But afterward I'm going straight back to the Larsens' to take a bath."

Nancy turned up the long drive that led to Vaughn Outfitters. Dana's van was parked in front of the A-frame. Nancy was surprised to see that Dana was still sitting in her van.

Dana got out of the van as soon as she saw Nancy. "*Now* what happened to you?"

"Don't ask," Nancy said. "Why were you waiting in the van? Isn't Lucas here?"

"He's here all right. I thought if I went in on my own, we'd only start arguing again. So I decided to wait for you."

Dana led the way into the office. Lucas was sitting behind his desk, entering figures into a ledger. He looked up and saw Dana first. "Now what?" he asked wearily. "Are you here to tell me that you've had my hunting license revoked?" Then his eyes fell on Nancy. "What on earth . . . ?"

"I'm fine," Nancy said. "It's just soot."

"Lucas," Dana began, "we came here because we need your help. Jesse is missing."

"It's more than that," Nancy added. "We now

137

know his brother is Alex Catlin—one of the escaped convicts. He's the one who's been sabotaging the refuge. There's a good chance he's after Jesse."

Dana handed the map to Lucas. "I found this in the cottage. We think he may be in one of the places circled here. Can you tell us exactly where they are?"

Lucas took the map without argument. He looked at it quickly and pointed to the circled area closest to the bottom of the map. "This is a cliff where bighorn sheep like to hang out. This one"—his finger moved higher on the map—"is a rock overhang where, if you're very lucky, you can spot a mountain lion or two. The third is a place where the red-tailed hawks like to nest." He looked impressed. "That boy would make a good guide. He knows the mountains and the animals."

"What's in the fourth circle?" Nancy asked.

Lucas arched one brow. "This one's a little different," he said. "It's an abandoned hunting lodge."

"Do you think he would hide out there?" Nancy asked.

Lucas frowned. "It's been a couple of years since I was inside. The place isn't in great shape, but it's probably better than a lean-to in the rain."

Nancy looked at Dana. "You know Jesse best. Do

you think he might be there—or in any of these other places?"

Dana hesitated before answering. "I'm not sure. But if he's hiding from his brother, the lodge seems most likely."

"She's right," Lucas said. "The other places are too open."

"Okay," Dana said, taking the map back. "How do we get there?"

"I take you there, that's how!" Lucas answered.

"Oh, no," Dana said. "The last thing I want—"

"You don't have a choice," Lucas interrupted. "Your brother would kill me if he ever found out I'd let you go after a convict on your own."

"Look," Nancy said quickly, "the important thing is finding Jesse. If Lucas knows where the lodge is and he's willing to lead us there, I think we should accept his offer."

Dana stared at the floor, and Lucas stood up. "I'm going to put together a few supplies," he said. "It'll take about ten minutes." He looked at Nancy and winked. "Do you think you could take a shower in that amount of time?"

"Definitely," Nancy answered. She followed Lucas upstairs.

"Wait a second," he said, disappearing into what she guessed was a bedroom. He emerged a few seconds later and tossed her a flannel shirt, a pair of dark green cords, and a pair of socks. "They might be big, but they're clean," he said.

Nancy gasped when she saw her reflection in the bathroom mirror. She wasted no time in hopping into the shower and scrubbing herself clean.

Ten minutes later, wearing Lucas's huge clothing, she came downstairs. Dana and Lucas were at it once again. Dana was gesturing angrily at the mounted animal heads. "I just want you to know that this is the most repulsive decor I have ever seen!"

"I'm sure it is," Lucas murmured. He was loading a rifle.

"Do you have to bring that?" Nancy asked.

"Dana thinks we may run into Alex Catlin," Lucas said evenly. "He's probably armed. I'm not about to chance meeting him unarmed. Bad odds."

"Let's find Jesse before Alex does," Nancy said, heading for the door.

Dusk was falling as Nancy trailed Lucas and Dana up yet another mountainside. In her right hand Nancy held a heavy flashlight that Lucas had given her. It was still too light to use it. She hoped they'd find the lodge before dark.

For the first time, she paid no attention to the splendor of the Rockies. All of her attention was concentrated on following Lucas Vaughn. Lucas, she was learning, was not an easy man to follow. There was no trail, but he never hesitated. He moved swiftly up the mountain with the ease of an animal. If he hadn't stopped often to make sure she was there, she would have lost him long ago.

Dana, who was used to the altitude, had no trouble keeping up. Nancy detached herself from a sticker bush. Why was it, she wondered, that Lucas and Dana never walked into sticker bushes?

It was almost dark when they caught sight of the abandoned hunting lodge. Built with thick timbers, it sat high on top of a ridge. The front steps were broken and the roof half-caved in.

"Terrific," Lucas muttered. "If he's in there and his brother hasn't shot him yet, he'll die of the architecture."

Nancy shivered. The lodge reminded her of the Midnight Mine. She'd already been through one cave-in today, and that was more than enough.

Lucas turned to Dana and Nancy. "You two stay put," he said quietly. "I'm going to circle around the lodge and see if anyone's in there." He set off without waiting for a response.

Dana immediately started after him. "I've had enough of you giving orders."

"Dana!" Nancy called. "Don't—"

But Dana was soon out of earshot, and Nancy

knew she couldn't call her back. Besides, she was still winded from the climb.

Cautiously, Nancy approached the lodge on her own. There were no lights inside, but she hadn't expected there to be working electricity. Was Jesse here at all? she wondered.

The woods were growing darker. Dana and Lucas were nowhere to be seen. Nancy felt her uneasiness grow with every minute. "Jesse?" she called softly.

A low laugh behind her caused Nancy to jump.

"I'll take that," said a strange man's voice. The heavy flashlight was removed from her hand.

Nancy whirled to face a tall, fair-haired man, wearing a long coat and holding a rifle. "I believe you're looking for me," said Alex Catlin. He shook his head in mock pity. "You would have done better to stay where I left you." He motioned her toward the lodge. "Inside."

15

Brothers

With the gun pressing against her back, Nancy stepped into the abandoned hunting lodge. A single candle lit the dark room. Nancy's heart sank as she saw Jesse sitting in a corner, his hands and feet bound.

"Jesse, are you all right?" Nancy cried.

"He's fine," Alex replied. "He's just beginning to pay the price for sending his brother to prison."

"I've paid for it every day since the trial," Jesse said quietly.

"No," Alex said. "You have no idea of how bad it's going to be."

"What are you going to do?" Jesse asked, his voice filled with contempt. "Kill us both? Have you killed anyone yet, Alex, or am I going to be the first?"

Alex lifted the gun from the small of Nancy's back and pushed her roughly to the floor. He stared at her, his eyes glittering in the candlelight. "I tried not to hurt you, girl. I left you alive on that mountain. Why couldn't you have stayed out of my way?"

One thing was clear to Nancy. She *had* gotten in the way. What Alex wanted was to hurt Jesse. She'd have to distract him, at least until she came up with a better plan. She forced herself to keep the fear out of her voice. "Why are you doing this?" she asked. "And why have you been threatening Jesse all along?"

"I wanted to get a message to my little brother," Alex replied. "I wanted him to know I'd found him. I wanted him to squirm."

"And that's why you released the bear and set that fire?" Nancy asked.

"I wanted my brother to feel fear," Alex said. His voice was cold. Nancy wondered if it had ever held any warmth.

"You know, Alex," Jesse said, "even fear gets worn-out after a while. You kept sending me those notes from prison. You were going to get me, your buddies on the outside were going to get me. . . . I believed them."

144

"Smart boy," Alex said. "You know I don't lie."

"You had me so terrified that I stole five hundred dollars so I could get away from you. For the past year I've lived like a fugitive, sure that someone was going to turn me in, or worse—tell *you* where I was."

"And then I found you," Alex said.

Jesse began to laugh softly. "You found me, all right. The weird thing was, by then I didn't have any fear left. Do what you want, Alex. You won't scare me anymore."

"You," Alex said to Nancy. "Sit by him. I'm out of rope, so I'm going to have to keep the gun on both of you."

Slowly, Nancy stood up and walked over to Jesse. At a nod from Alex, she sat down beside him. Where were Dana and Lucas? she wondered. The only thing she could do was keep Alex talking. "What are you going to do with me? The police in Seven Rocks know where I am," she bluffed. "I left word before I came up here."

At that moment, something struck the outside of the lodge. Alex looked up sharply.

The object struck again.

This time Alex cursed. The one window in the lodge was on the opposite side of the long, empty room. Keeping his gun trained on Nancy and Jesse, Alex backed toward the window. It was covered with some sort of greasy paper. He punched the end of the rifle through the paper and leaned out the window, pointing the gun into the darkness.

Then he spun suddenly, advancing on Nancy and Jesse. "Don't try anything," he warned. He jumped as something else hit the outside of the lodge.

"What's wrong?" Jesse taunted his brother. "Getting nervous?"

Nancy was sure that either Dana or Lucas was responsible for whatever was hitting the lodge. And Alex was getting more upset by the minute. Would that help them or make him even more dangerous than he already was?

"It seems we have company," Alex said to Nancy. "You didn't come up here alone, did you?"

"I told you," Nancy said calmly. "The police know I'm here."

"Well, they're taking their sweet time about rescuing you," Alex scoffed. He leaned back against the wall. He was playing a kind of game with the rifle, floating it back and forth so that at any moment either Jesse or Nancy appeared in its sight. "You missed my last act," he told his brother. "I left a present for that mountain lion you're so fond of. It should be dead by now."

"What are you talking about?" Jesse demanded.

"Poison," Alex replied. "I left poisoned meat for the cat. It ate it all."

For the first time, Jesse fought wildly against his bonds.

"Don't!" Nancy warned. "That's exactly what he wants." Jesse shut his eyes and stopped struggling.

"The mountain lion is dead!" Alex jeered. He was watching his brother with something close to glee.

"But it's not," Nancy said quickly, although she wasn't sure whether that was true. "Dana got to the cat right away. It's unconscious, but it's alive."

Two heavy objects hit the outside of the lodge. This time, Alex reacted with split-second reflexes. He fired directly through the wall of the building at the source of the sound.

He's terrified, Nancy realized. She would have to gamble on his fear.

"There!" she cried hysterically. She pointed to the end of the lodge, her face a mask of fear. Her voice rose to a scream. "It's coming in through the window!"

Alex whirled to face the window, his gun raised.

"Put the gun down, Catlin," Lucas Vaughn said calmly. He stood in the doorway, his rifle trained on Alex's back. Alex whirled again, ready to shoot.

"That's not a good idea." Lucas's voice was deadly quiet. "Kick the gun away, and turn around with your hands to the wall."

For the longest moment, Alex stood motionless. His eyes were fixed on Lucas, as if he were silently

147

asking Lucas whether or not he'd really shoot. Something must have convinced him Lucas would. Alex dropped the gun, kicked it away, and put his hands up against the wall.

Dana walked in a second later, carrying Lucas's pack. "My rock idea worked!"

"Would you mind cutting these ropes?" Jesse asked with a touch of his old impatience.

"Delighted," Dana said. She pulled a knife from the pack and freed him.

"Just save enough to tie up Alex," said Lucas.

"Bess." George shook her cousin's shoulder. "It's a gorgeous day, and we're finally going hiking. Don't you want to get up?"

"No," Bess mumbled, and turned away.

"Let her sleep," Nancy said, laughing. "After all, she did manage to straighten out my account with Nellie."

"Right," George said, grinning. "It must have been exhausting."

Downstairs in the kitchen, Cal and Maggie were eating breakfast. Nancy and George had no sooner joined them than the doorbell rang.

"Now what?" Cal asked, going to the door. He winked at Nancy. "Didn't you tell me your case was solved?"

Before Nancy could assure him that it was, Dana

and Jesse walked into the room. "We just wanted to make sure Nancy's okay," Dana said.

"You must join us for breakfast," Maggie said. Dana accepted at once, and Jesse, looking unsure, sat down as well.

"How's the mountain lion?" Nancy asked.

"She's going to be okay," Jesse said with one of his rare smiles. "Either Dana's first aid worked or Alex didn't use enough poison. The cat regained consciousness this morning. She even stood up."

"And the bear is his usual bad-tempered self. I think we're going to release the mountain lion cub next week, too," Dana reported happily.

The doorbell rang again. Cal raised his eyebrows. A few minutes later, he returned with Sergeant Baker and Lucas Vaughn.

"I knew it," Dana said, burying her head in her arms. "I can't escape him."

"And good morning to you, too, Miss Walsh," Lucas said, laughing.

"We are going to have a pleasant breakfast," Maggie declared, bringing a large bowl of fresh fruit to the table. "That means you two will observe a truce while you are in my kitchen. Is that clear?"

Looking a bit sheepish, Dana and Lucas nodded and smiled at each other.

"Maggie, you're amazing," said Sergeant Baker.

"Even I can't keep the peace as well as you can."
Everyone at the table laughed.

George turned to the police officer. "Is Alex 'The Cat' Catlin safely behind bars?"

"Yes," Sergeant Baker replied, "for a long, long time. He confessed to everything that happened up at Paws, as well as to leaving the trap on the porch and stealing the truck and the rifle."

"What I want to know is how he got away with kidnapping Nancy on Gaslight Night while just about everyone in Seven Rocks was out on the streets," Cal said. "He sure pulled one over on Harry."

"Well, he fit right in, wearing that long coat," Sergeant Baker said. "Alex had been watching the comings and goings at Paws, and he knew that Nancy was getting closer and closer to the truth. So he kidnapped her and left her on the mountain."

Nancy saw a brief flash of pain in Jesse's eyes. For the first time, she realized how much it must have cost him to testify against his brother.

A sleepy-eyed Bess arrived at the table in a flowing pink silk robe. "What's going on?" she asked. "I heard you all from the third floor!"

"We're celebrating the recapture of Alex Catlin and the good health of the bear, the mountain lion, and the cub. Not to mention the temporary truce between Lucas and Dana," said Maggie.

"Not to mention laying to rest Phineas Josiah Armbruster's ghost," added Cal.

Bess smiled and went to the refrigerator.

"Where did you get that robe?" George asked her cousin.

"Nellie's, of course," said Bess, striking a pose. "It's where I plan to do all my shopping."

Everyone was in high spirits, and breakfast flew by quickly. Surprisingly, Jesse was the last to leave. "Could I talk to you for a minute?" he said to Nancy.

"Sure," Nancy answered in surprise.

Together they walked out onto the veranda.

"I was pretty nasty to you," he said quickly. "I just wanted to apologize for some of the things I said."

"You weren't all that awful," Nancy assured him, smiling. She held out her hand. "Friends?"

Jesse grinned and gave her hand a quick shake. "Friends."

Munro twined around her ankles as Nancy watched Jesse go down the walk. I never would have believed it, she thought. Then she reached down, scooped up the cat, and headed back into the house.

NANCY DREW® MYSTERY STORIES By Carolyn Keene

A MINSTREL® BOOK

Published by Pocket Books